A Piece of Me

Jermaine Smith

A Piece of Me

ISBN 978-0-578-12192-5

Library of Congress Control Number: 2013938611

Front Cover Photo: Kris Rios for La Productions Photography

Back Cover Photo: PhotosbyKai

Cover Design: William Lee

This book is dedicated to my sons
Kyree J. Smith and Tristan G. Henson-Smith.
I love you both and I thank God every day for the
blessings that you both have been to me. I love you two
more than you could ever know.

Acknowledgments

I would like to thank my mother Sonia and my sister Tiffany for surviving through our initial part of this journey we call life. The road was rough, unexpected but designed to bring us to this day. Thanks you to my grandmother Melissa (RIP) and my aunt Darlene for always encouraging me to push forward and to not focus on the things that I could not change.

Thank you to all of my family members who have supported my dreams and have taken the time to say a prayer for me. There are too many of you to name. Thanks to all of my friends that also dream chase and have pushed forward pass their obstacles.

Thanks to every actor and friend who has practiced their craft and shared their talents or time with "A Piece of Me" the stage play when it was in production.

Thank you to every school teacher that has ever written on a chalkboard for me to learn from. You are appreciated.

Finally, I would like to thank my partner and best friend who encouraged me daily and pushed me to make this next step of life with this book a reality, Ms. Yolanda Moore.

Table of Contents

The Condom Was Right There

It was a strangely warm Sunday morning in late January. I say it was strange because it was almost two weeks before February and I still could wear my light over coat. I was sitting in my wife Maxine's church with my coat draped over my arm, as I shifted around preparing myself to hear the word as the sun bounced off my face. As always, I managed to get the seat that I usually sat in when I did come to church, which was in the over flow area in the back. I was with some familiar faces because I sat where most of the visitors, talkers and late comers who routinely liked to leave early. The latter was my group of choice. I would cut out in a heartbeat. I was just not one for the extended services and the three or four different offerings. My wife loved and accepted me. She never judged me. She accepted me for me. Maxine knew that I loved and prayed to God but I was not one for organized religion. I just couldn't see the growth in the people from the times that I did come. They wore the same clothes, they had the same complaints and some had the worst attitudes. There is nothing worse than a person with a title in a church with an attitude. I definitely couldn't understand why the same member who would cry broke, still would give up their last few dollars to a church that showed they had more than them. It always made me question who's faith was stronger- the pastor, who obviously knows how much tithe and offering is flowing into the church every month or the members who may or may not have a job and are trying to figure out how they're going to pay their rent, but every time the church doors open they are there. These same church folks who whispered about me not being a good husband for not coming to church with my wife are the same church folks who claim to be so holy and in love with a God they can't see or touch. I learned from my mother a longtime ago that everybody comes to church for different reasons. Many come for God, some come for man, and the rest come to see who they can see. I say they're just here for attendance. I would watch people do extra walking up and down the aisles to be seen. Mama always said that the church is like the hospital, everyone came in sick, but not everybody leaves healed. I knew in my heart that I was in need of some healing and today was an extra special day for my wife. This was the second year that she and the Ladies of Faith were in charge of coordinating the annual Women's Day service. The Ladies of Faith was a group of female leaders from the church that included the first lady, most of the mothers of the church, a few deaconesses, some head ushers and selective members. My wife would often tell me how they needed this year's program to be a good one. To me that meant they needed it to be more profitable. Apparently, attendance has been low at the Women's Day event for the past few years. She always heard the ten years ago stories of how successful those services were compared to the ones of late. I told her it was a reflection of the economy and not the new leadership. Maxine worked night after night for the past three months all for this one day. She was extremely proud of the program that they had put together that included praise dancers, the mass choir, a surprise award dinner, and a guest speaker that she said I just had to see. I was surprised to see that they went with a male preacher for this year's event. Maxine told me how all of the other ladies on the committee objected because this was going against tradition. Every Women's Day service in the past featured a female speaker or preacher, so this year was definitely different.

I knew in my soul that I had to be in church this Sunday to support her, but there was a more pressing reason for me to be there too. It was riding up my spine that less than twenty four hours ago I was sitting in an abortion clinic with a woman that I had been cheating with for the past two years. I sat in that abortion clinic thinking how much I didn't know about this woman and just how far gone I was.

I sat in the pew with my navy blue pinstriped suit looking down at my brown shoes with my face in my hands the same way I sat in that clinic just yesterday. "How did I get here?" I thought to myself. "How did I allow myself to get this woman pregnant when the condom was right there in my pants pocket?" I was fighting my conscience. I was fighting with the consequences of coming clean and I was trying to prepare myself mentally to block out every word that was going to be preached this morning. I got snatched out of my daze every other minute by someone either saying "It's good to see you on this Sunday morning Brother Bryce" or "Brother Bryce your wife asked me to escort you to the front". I got so tired of fake smiling that I just put my head down and focused on the program that I had clenched in my left hand. I pretended not to hear anyone talking to me.

I just wanted to zone out and hear from God, not the preacher, and definitely not any of the ushers. I was scared, lost and disconnected all at the same time. I was a wreck. But I was in the house of God and it would take God, Jesus, and all the angels of heaven to help me now.

I knew it was just a matter of time before Maxine would come to get me herself, and there would be no telling her no so I just went ahead and got up the minute I heard the lady next to me say "Brother Bryce, here comes your wife". As I grabbed my coat, my church program fell right along with my phone and my bible. My phone and all of its parts went everywhere, and so did all the papers that I had stuck in between my bible pages. My notes, napkins, and about ten tithing envelopes flew under the row in front of me. As I kneeled down to pick everything up, I came face-to-face with a pair of three inch silver studded red bottom Christian Louboutin heels that were perfectly attached to the size seven feet of my beautiful wife. She was five feet eight, petite, with long jet black hair and an hour glass shaped body to match. She was definitely eye candy. I took as long as I could to pick up all of my stuff trying my best to prolong this walk to the front. I quickly stuck everything back in my bible. When I looked up, I saw that my wife had my coat in one hand and her other hand out to help me up. I put my hand into hers and pulled up on the back of the back of the seat in front of me.

She pulled me close to her and whispered softly, "I see all them tithing envelopes, somebody must've been just putting in the offering only."

I had a few choice words for her swirling in my head, but all I could do at that moment was just smile as she grabbed my hand and we walked almost side by side to the front of the church. I was a few paces behind as I tried to look at as many people as possible. I could feel every eye in the church on me from the balcony, to the choir stand, all the way down to the front pew. But what was funny was that I couldn't hear the choir that was right in front of me singing away. It was like the sound in my head just went out. Everybody to my right and to my left was standing up singing and clapping by the time we got to the front of the church. I felt like I was some big time celebrity who was being sneaked into the church. I couldn't hunch my shoulders any lower or walk any faster to try to get to my seat or I would have tripped me and Maxine both. Once we finally got to the pew, I made it my business to sit down and get myself together while everyone else was standing. My heart was racing and it felt like I had just ran a few miles on the treadmill. My palms and forehead were sweaty and my left hand would not stop shaking. I was already uncomfortable sitting in the over flow section. I knew I had no chance of enjoying the service from where I was sitting now. I couldn't play with my phone sitting this close to the pastor. There would be no reading of the program over and over and over to see how much time we had left. And leaving early was definitely out of the question. I was in a bird's eye view of all the pastors and deacons who sat off to the side in the pulpit as the guest speaker began to speak and thank all of those who brought him in for today's service. He honored the "Angel of the House", the congregation, and he thanked his own church members who came to support him. Of course, he couldn't forget to thank his lovely wife who sat just three seats away from me in her sky blue and white St. John's suit with the hat to match. I felt like I was positioned on purpose, literally and figuratively, to hear from God. Yet, I was still looking for a reason not to be.

I had to admit that my usual bravado was completely gone and the coward on the inside of me automatically took over. At this point, the only thing I knew to do was open my bible and stare at the page. If anyone was watching me and they could see the real me all they would see was a nervous coward staring at his bible crying on the inside. I gazed down into my bible to where I could only see the top of the page and the feet of the choir members as they walked back to their seats. This could mean only one thing; that the pastor was about to start his sermon and my wife was on her way back to her seat.

And, on cue, she walked right over and sat down next to me while gently touching my neck.

"Are you okay babe?" she asked as she looked directly into my eyes.

"Yes." I said as I raised my head and glanced towards the pastor as he started to sing the last song that Maxine had just led the choir with.

Maxine now placed her hand on mine motioning for me to sit up. This is when I started to get hit with line after line from the pastor and seemingly picked apart in my seat as the Pastor said "If two things or people coming together do not enhance each other and highlight each other's strength, then those two things should not come together." He also added that "A marriage without God in it is nothing but an arrangement."

My throat felt like it was closing up on me and it felt like the room was getting smaller. I needed some air. I needed an escape from my own lies, my own denial, and it was at that moment the pastor said, "Before there can be a resurrection, there first has to be a cross."

I'm not the most spiritual person, but I was in awe by the delivery, timing and the accuracy of the pastor's words, especially with everything that was beating me down at the moment. Not only did his words hit me, but I also got swallowed up by the uproar of cries and praise that were let out from the congregation as the pastor continued to preach on. Everyone around me was now in either a second or third gear and was moving with God. I definitely felt like God was in the room with us right then. I was ready to cry, I was ready to run. I was ready to give in to my pain, but no part of me was going to get up and dance like everyone else. I was never one to show any outward emotion and I was not about to start today. I was good at concealing my hurts and pain, but I felt right now was the time for me to begin to stop suffering in silence and to open up to Maxine. I knew for certain that she married me for my potential and not my reality. She always encouraged me and told me what I could become if I just opened up and lived more. So I know I needed to start this journey by telling her that I was unfaithful. I had to convince myself that I was fully broken, detached and in limbo of how to give all my wrongs to God. I was cornered and ready to release, but I didn't know how to deal with my situation. How do I take me out of the situation and make it all about God? I asked myself. How can things ever be the same with us? Will they? How do I tell my wife that I stepped out on her and got some woman pregnant? Everything seemed to spiral so quickly. Everything around me was still closing in and all the sound went back on mute. I could not hear the musicians leading the praise break, nor could I hear the hand claps of the people sitting right next to me. I could see the members crying with their arms raised, but no sound. I then began to feel the constant bumps from my wife as she was in full praise mode while running back and forth between the aisle and her seat. I wanted her near me but I was not going to move from my seat to get her attention as she danced in the circle that was formed by five others around her. I couldn't make eye contact with her, so I sat back and put my head down to try and hear from God. I wiped my forehead several times with the last two good napkins that I had left in my inside suit pocket. Every other napkin met with a crumbled fate or eventually fell apart on my face as I used it. It was then that I felt some fingers run smoothly over my hands that were placed on my head. I looked up and saw Maxine standing over me smiling and crying, I felt my ears pop and all of a sudden I heard the pastor in a loud crisp and clear voice say, "One day you will realize that some people can stay in your heart, but not in your life."

By this time the building had become an all-out praise party. My wife, the guest pastor's wife, and the entire row all jumped up and moved as if they were forever set free. I knew I looked out of place because I felt it. It was taking everything in me to not get up and leave. My mind and eyes were looking at all the exits, but my heart and gut were telling me to stay with God. It was escape time and all I needed was the right opportunity. I was certain that today was the wrong day to tell Maxine about my infidelity. I figured it may be better to try to preserve what we have rather than to try regain what we've already lost. It didn't make sense to disturb what she may feel is an above average decent home. We all have our relation-ship issues in life that we must fight through. Maxine deserves better than me. She should not be a victim caught in my path as I hesitate to mature. I really messed up this time and I know I won't be able to soothe it over by simply cooking dinner or taking her shopping. My mind was in full cover up mode looking for some way to justify my actions. This was me. This is who I am.

I was sitting front and center in the church on the front row and all I could think of in my mind was that none of this would be happening now if I would've just put a condom on. I took myself back to the moment and could literally see that the condom was within reach in my pants. With everything going on around me I still had a clear visual of my pants lying across the end of the bed. All I had to do was grab them, reach in my pocket and take one out. Sitting in the midst of this praise break and all that I could somehow hear were the voices of my friends talking about how they wouldn't be caught up in child support or in their unwanted marriages if they would have just put a condom on. I was always the voice of reason for the group, but yet I could never seem to overpower my own lies. I still carry all of my childhood wounds around with me, but this unexpected pregnancy and abortion only added to the problems Maxine and I already had. The weight of it all brought me to a point where God was my last resort, yet I can't commit even though I am in the best position to start over.

It seems I cannot shake lying to myself or to stop fronting as if I was this super strong person that does not mess up. The one thing that should be the easiest is turning out to be the hardest. My not being able to open up to myself or not allowing anyone in that could pull me away from my inner pain was doing more and more damage every moment that I fought it. I always brushed to the back of my head the thought of taking this hurt from my childhood to my wife because I didn't want her to view me as the weak or unstable man that I truly was. I could live with her not knowing who she truly married until I built up the strength to let her deeper under the surface of those issues. I always wanted my wife to view me as a man of integrity. I never had the share and confide in me with anything talks with my mother as a child or with either of my sisters, Darlene and Sheryl as adults. Our baby brother Joseph came well behind us and was more like our child than a brother because we fed, bathed and took him with us everywhere we went. The only outlet that I really had was my friends that I hung out with and these were the same friends that I could not go to and tell about my latest screw up because I knew that a few of them had their eyes on Maxine. And at no point was I about to give any of them any ammunition to help seal the deal and get her; not that I believed my wife would step out on me anyway. I know in my heart that she was too good of a Christian and too in love with me to even consider such a thing. It was me who chose to live the fake it until you make it lifestyle. As much as I hated to admit it, I had the same logic as the old man who laid around the house when we were kids being forced to go to church. He demanded that my mother keep him away from her church rhetoric, its dealings and its folks. Maybe it was me and my opinion of how my wife and the other members seem to hold the pastor in a higher regard than Jesus Christ himself. They would drop everything that they had going on if he called or if they heard he needed something. To this day I can't understand how twenty women sitting in a church can all say that God told them that pastor was their husband. "Either the twenty of them had to be wrong or there were nineteen of them that could not be hearing correctly from God." I would joke to Maxine about the ladies in her church.

As I sat there waiting for the service to end, I realized that the joke was possibly on me because I might end up losing my wife because of my cheating and immature ways. So, here I was sitting proudly side by side with my wife and it felt like everyone sitting around us and everyone that touched the microphone today had looked straight through me. For years I let the assumed thoughts of these people keep me away from this church. I questioned Maxine if these people only liked me because they loved her or did they love me because it's what the scriptures command them to do. She claimed that they loved me as they loved God, but they always made me feel uneasy when I did come to the church. I felt the pressure of my wife wanting me here so badly and I often heard from her about the pressures she felt for being in a leadership role and her husband never being present by her side in service. I looked at the people around us and at the other people who I knew were in leadership, as well as those who sat behind the pastor as he began to close. Maxine reached down to her right to nudge me up as the pastor had asked everyone to stand. As I stood, I could hear the pastor say "We will now have our altar call and open up the doors to the church." My heart and mind immediately started to race again as my wife decided to slide her hand into mine as my fingers got cold and numb. My mind was on getting through the crowded aisles of the church once the service was over and bypassing the unwanted after service conversations. I just wanted to leave. I knew I wasn't ready to be prayed for, nor was I willing to start my road to recovery today. I heard the invite from the pastor saying to just try God, but my feet wouldn't move the same way my heart wouldn't commit. All of this as my wife held and squeezed my hand back to warmth and to comfort me. It seemed as if she knew everything that was going on inside of me, but she was leaving it up to me to figure out. My guilt was working overtime now as I watched my wife wipe away tear after tear from her face for almost the last two hours. It was no coincidence that the pastor had just said to us all "You've done all that you can do now leave it up to Jesus".

Once the pastor said that, a loud scream for God's mercy was heard coming from the back of the church. This one cry set off a chain reaction of crying and praising for about another two minutes that felt more like fifteen. But the pastor told the musicians about two or three times to don't even get started as they tapped the drums and the keys on the organ. He then told the congregation that, "We cannot dance our way into heaven, but that we have to get back to getting on our knees and talking to God, as that has become a lost art."

It was then that I looked at Maxine as she fanned herself while pacing the aisle. I said to myself that I didn't deserve her and that it was time I really considered fixing me. She used both of her hands and pulled me close to her to whisper to me to wait for the benediction before walking out. She either saw it in my face or she could tell by my body language that I already had one foot out the door. As she grabbed my left hand I stood back up to hear the final words. The service was over and the pastor left the congregation with the instructions for the week and they were for everyone to see how "Our lessons are always in our failures, but our understanding is in our successes".

Now with this word I should've felt more empowered and compelled to do the right thing, but I felt more and more like a failure who couldn't tell his wife that he had a nine o'clock appointment yesterday morning at an abortion clinic, not a Saturday morning workout with friends like I wrote in the note I left. If the Lord could just help me own my life and free me from being a slave to my habits, I just know that my marriage could work. I was living a life full of excuses, and my life, my wife and my marriage deserved better. I learned from today's service that the righteous don't always prosper and the wicked don't always suffer.

The Ride Home

As I sat in my truck listening to the sports station, I watched member after member come out of the church to stand around and socialize. It was as if no one wanted to go home. It was maybe fifteen or twenty minutes after service had ended and there was still no sign of my wife. It made no sense for me to get mad because this was the usual whenever I did come to church and we drove one car. The only thing I could do was get comfortable. I reached on the side of the seat to hit the recline button and lay back comfortably since I was going to be waiting for awhile. As soon I placed my head back onto the head rest, I could see Leah's face. Leah was around Maxine's height and complexion but she was Dominican and a whole lot thicker in the body with hair falling all the way down her back. She had a smile that would just cripple you. Her eyebrows were always cut precisely to go with her designer shades that she would never stepped outside without. I loved her shoe game, her walk, and the way her calves embraced her stockings when she wore them. Leah never failed to tell me how much she loved my brown chocolate skin tone and jet black ceasar haircut that matched so perfectly as she would say it. She always slowly took off my suit and said how difficult it was for her to undress me because of how fit and well cut my clothes laid over my body. She understood that she could not wear any of her fragrances around me for the fear of me going home with her scent on, but she loved leaving our rendevouz smelling like the Jean Paul Gaultier cologne that she bought for me. These meet ups were the perfect remedies from my job as a computer programmer at K&T Global and from my wife. Even though Leah had the greatest personality and was supposed to be only fun, I was very much attracted to her. Now after two years of fun we found ourselves in an abortion clinic with nothing to laugh about. We were more divided than I would have ever imagined. We should never have hooked up in the first place. We came to the clinic both knowing for certain that this was a child that we could not have, would not have, but as we sat through the paperwork and over heard some of the conversations and read the body language of the other woman (mostly girls), there was a change of heart brewing from her as each conversation from her would began with a sympathetic look. The entire room was caught off guard by one young girl's outburst to a woman that appeared to be her mother. She jumped up and screamed out, "You not going to make me do this. This is my baby! This is my life!" Everyone in the room was looking in their direction and listening in. The young girl then grabbed her coat and scarf from the lady and walked out. Everyone watched with anticipation as the lady got up and threw the clipboard onto the counter of the admission desk and walked out behind the girl. All you could hear was a room full of side conversations and arguments. As Leah looked at me, I told her with a straight face "Don't even think about it. Don't even think about changing your mind."

"I don't know if I could go through with this. I don't feel good about this and I'm starting to feel weak." Leah said as she looked at me with some saddened glassy eyes while running her hand back and forth through her hair.

"You're feeling weak because you couldn't eat after midnight. Trust me everything will be alright and we can grab something to eat as soon as we leave." I replied to her as I took off of my Adidas track suit jacket to get comfortable and to show her that we were not leaving.

"No! Everything will not be alright because you can go right back to your family life once this is all done." she said with a sharp nasty tone as if this feeling had been on her mind for weeks.

"Yes that is true, but have I done that? Have I left you abandoned you? Who is here with you now? Where is your family?"

"My family didn't get me pregnant. You did!" she said without once blinking and pointing her finger at me.

"Look Leah we are here and we are going to take care of business. Besides you were the one who said that you didn't want any children and that if it ever came down to it, you would never have a child with me that you would have to hide. So tell me now what has changed and tell me how the hell do you think that we can we work?" I whispered angrily to her face as I leaned over to her so that our conversation could remain between us.

"It's not a matter of how can it work, but it is a matter of who will be the one in that room laying on that table alone. It is a matter of me living with this decision for the rest of my life, not you. We both know that you only came here to make sure that this abortion gets done." she said as she brought her face closer to mines as the tears started to form in her eyes.

"I can't believe that you would even say that to me. I can't believe that you would even put me in the category of someone who would just show up to make sure that an abortion is done." I said as now turned my entire body towards her in my seat while putting my fingertip on her stomach.

Just as our debate was heating up, one of the assistants called her name so that she could go to the back and get prepped. As she handed me her pocket book, phone and coat she said "Pray for me". I could see she was scared. And we never had the type of relationship, situation or connection between us where she could ask me to pray for her. I wanted to tell her to come back, let's leave, but I couldn't. Who would have known that this would be last time that I would watch her walk away from me. I had no clue as I sat there for hours and hours watching every other woman that came in after us go in to have the procedure done and come back out with no sign of her. I kept saying that I would ask one of the staffers if everything was alright with her in the back and if she would be coming out soon, but I brushed it off and gave it another five to ten minutes each time and waited. Those five to ten minutes added up and it was now three hours later and I wrote off the fact that maybe she needed a cooling off period for her body, so I said that I was going to ask the next patient who came out of the back if they had seen her. I didn't really want to approach anyone as they just left the back, but all the people who came in with us were now either in the back or had left already. It was just me and the television out in the reception area. As I got up to go get what was left of the newspaper from on the seat across from me, I heard a man's voice call me from the same door that all the patients had been entering into that led to the back of the clinic.

"Sir, are you waiting for Ms. Carver?" the gentleman asked in a cool calm voice as he pushed on the wall mounted hand sanitizer to get some out for his hands.

"I don't know a Ms. Carver and I'm waiting for Leah Ramos." I replied as I sat up to the edge of the chair to turn towards him.

"Okay. Well did you happen to see anyone else waiting out here for someone?" he asked as he stood with one leg in the door and rubbing in the sanitizer on his hands.

"No. But can you possibly help me because I have been out here waiting for my friend for the last few hours and no one has come out to tell me if she is okay or how much longer that she would need to recover." I asked as I grabbed my jacket and Leah's belongings off of the seat right next to me.

"I apologize for that but we only have one young lady remaining back here and we need to speak to whoever has accompanied her."

"How does she look?"

"She's a short fair skinned woman with long hair." he said as he demonstrated her height with his hands.

"That's my Leah." I said to him as I got up to walk around the rows of chairs while dropping what was left of the newspaper that had been sitting on my lap.

"Sir what's your name?" he asked as he let the door close and begin to walk towards me.

"It's Bryce, I mean Brian."

"Bryce, Brian whatever, I need you to come identify this young lady. Do you have identification on you?"

"Of course I have ID. What do you mean identify? I came here with a Leah Ramos. Who is this Ms. Carver?" I asked as I stepped over the newspaper pages that now covered half of the row.

"Sir the young lady we have in the back wristband and chart says that her name is Janette Carver." he said as he looked at my driver's license that I passed him.

It was right then that I heard two loud knocks on my car window. It was one of the church members signaling to me to roll down the window.

"Brother Bryce your wife asked me to come over here to tell you that she will be out in about five minutes." Brother Carl said as I rolled the window down halfway to hear him.

"Thank you." I replied to him as he constantly looked over his shoulder at each passing car to make sure they weren't coming down the street too fast and too close.

"Be good my brother and I hope to see you at mid-week prayer." Brother Carl said as he back pedaled away from the truck.

"You just might." I replied and felt a sigh of relief that this was all that Brother Carl was coming to tell me because he can talk with the best of them.

"Be blessed my brother." Brother Carl shouted to me as he turned and walked off.

As I rolled the window back up, my eyes followed him as he walked back towards his post on the corner while stopping at a few cars that were double parked to talk for a second. While glancing back at the building I noticed that many of the church members were still standing around talking. I wondered what could be so important to these people to still be out here catching up.

I looked at groups and groups of people just laughing and talking it up as if no one felt the temperature beginning to drop. There was now a little breeze coming through that you could feel as I had the window cracked with the truck now turned off. Finally, out of the front church door comes Mrs. Max' with a few people in tow, so it was either time for some sidewalk talk for her or we were now dropping people off to their homes with me playing taxi. I was hoping that she didn't accept an invite to any after church quick meals or even pitch the idea to have one. Because if she did. She sure was going by herself. I was tired, confused and all churched out. There was no way that I was coming back for the second service or to the surprise award dinner tonight. I hit the recline button so that I could move the seat back up and get out to and go around the truck to open up the door for her, and as I got out to go around I heard her say.

"Don't worry I got it." Maxine said as she placed both her clutch and bible bag into her left hand. Not to mention that she had the I cannot wait to get these heels off face on.

"What's wrong?" I asked with curiosity so that I can gauge what type of ride home it would be for us.

"Everything is good." she replied as she walked straight to the back door.

"Why are you getting into the back?" I asked as I looked over the roof and then through the car at her to see what she was doing.

"I'm just putting my bible bag and my clutch on the back seat and I'm grabbing my flats that are back here on the floor." she said as she reached down behind the seat to pick up her Chinese looking slippers that she calls flats. I have been trying to get my hands on these slippers since last summer so that I could throw them away. Maxine would say that they were no longer pretty but they were still comfortable.

"Okay I was just asking because it took you awhile to come out." I said as I sat down in the driver's seat and watched her every move.

"Sorry about that. I texted you three times to tell you that I was in a meeting. I had to meet with the pastor and the Ladies of Faith real quick." she said as she closed the rear door and opened the passenger door to get in.

"My bad I had my phone on vibrate and I haven't looked at it since service ended."

"How did you enjoy the service?" she asked as she slid into the seat smiling at me and reaching over her shoulder to put on her seatbelt.

"Service was good. You know me." I replied as I grabbed the steering wheel and turned the key to start the engine.

"Yeah I know you." she said with a funny little smirk on her face that always meant it was about to be confrontation time.

"What does that mean?" I asked as I paused from putting on my seatbelt to hear her response.

"It means that I know you, and that church is not your thing."

"Max' look."

"Now is not the right time Bryce, nor is this the right place. Not in front of the church. So can you drive off." she said as she pointed towards the windshield for me to drive off while cracking her window because she always had to have air.

"Maxine, I'm not about to argue with you. I want you to enjoy your Sunday." I said as I clicked my seatbelt and checked my rearview and passenger side mirrors before pulling out.

"How about we enjoy our Sunday together?" she said as she slid off both of her heels to start massaging her feet.

"Yes you're right. Let's enjoy our Sunday together." I replied as I looked at her face and then glancing at her feet. Maxine knew that I did not like for her to have her feet on my seats. She was baiting me into an argument over what I appreciate more, her or my truck.

"Would you like to go and.."

"I would like nothing better than to go home and re-lax right now." I replied quickly and with my form of extreme sarcasm as she would put it before she could finish her sentence. Since everyone reminds me of how nasty my mouth is and how messed up my attitude is. I always tried to live up to the accusations.

"Bryce what is wrong with you? You are edgy and you keep cutting me off. How can you leave church and still have an attitude?" she said as she massaged each toe one by one with her heel hanging of the edge of the seat.

"I don't have an attitude."

"Well your actions say otherwise."

"Max', we are not in no movie or a rehearsal. So stop sounding like one of your movie scripts."

"Oh, so that's it. You have a problem with me being in between jobs." she said as she put her foot back down on the floor and turned almost her entire body to face me.

"No, I don't and I didn't say that."

"Bryce, I am an actress."

"I know what you do from time to time, you don't have to remind me, and you don't have to tell me that the work comes and goes. I can see that." I said to her without the thought of making any form of eye contact.

For years I've tried to get my wife to see that her best years of acting were behind her and still remain support-ive. She don't see how or is willing to accept that the phone calls for her to come read for roles have came to an end. She went from five or six readings a week to hardly two readings a month. All of her voiceover work has disappeared and she's paying a agent to get her into doors that she could get into on her own. When I do mention that she's wasting her time by now performing in local theater productions that she would have never considered before; I'm all of a sudden the bad guy.

"You're right I don't have to tell you because we have been married for over ten years and you know that this is the first time that I have ever gone more than six months without a gig." she said as I watched her in the rearview mirror rolling her eyes at the side of my head before shifting back forward in the seat.

"Exactly, and with the bills we have, six months is a long time for one person to pull all the weight."

"Pull all the weight? Bryce we are married. If one of us hits a rough patch then the other is supposed to hold it down until the other one gets back on their feet." she said as she placed the right side of her body against the door.

"I never said I had a problem holding it down. I just think that it's time that you consider looking for a regular job too." I said to her as I looked over at her as we sat at the red light.

"So that's what all of this attitude is about huh? You feel that you're doing it all?" she asked as she pulled the sun visor down to look into the mirror.

"I told you that I don't have no attitude."

"Yeah you do. That's why you were so uneasy in church today because of your selfish ways and your attitude." she said as she began to make teeth cleaning noises of food that was not there and folding a napkin that she took out of the glove compartment to start removing her eye-liner.

"Max' I don't have no attitude."

"Yeah, you do, and God cannot get through to you if you keep it up."

"Keep what up? Look, when I was younger it was my actions that moved me away from God, but I've fixed my attitude and now God is working on my actions." I replied as I stopped short of rear ending the car in front of us.

"Who do you think you're talking to Bryce King? I know you. You're as stubborn as your father, if not worse." she replied as she looked at the napkin and then back up at the mirror on the visor.

"Don't go there Maxine."

"Bryce when you decide to fully let God, me and everyone else who loves you into your heart, your faith will finally out grow your fears."

"How did you marry a man that you feel won't let you into his heart?"

"I accepted your marriage proposal because I love you and I knew that you loved me. Notice that I said I love you and not that I loved you because I still do."

"I know the difference. And why do you do that?" I asked as I gripped the steering wheel tighter with my left hand before hitting on the horn a few times at the slow moving cars that were in front of us.

"Do what?" she asked with her arms folded staring at me as if we never had this same discussion over a hundred times.

"Do that."

"I do it for the same reasons that you look to start arguments, Bryce!"

"I do not look to start arguments with you."

"Yeah, you right. Because you do it with everyone and not just me so I guess I shouldn't feel special." she said with her usual undertone gesture that always leads to how I don't separate her as a priority from anything or anyone else.

"You're special alright."

"Bryce, what do I do for you? Why do you still love me? Better yet, do you love me?" she asked as she put some final touches on her outside of church lipstick while pushing the visor back up.

"Well, I know one thing that you haven't done for me, and that is you helping me with these bills for the last six months." I replied as I looked into the rear view mirror to switch lanes.

"Bryce King, Do you know how much praying I do for you? How much praying I do for us?" she said to me as she placed her left hand on my leg.

"We can't write the words she praying for us on no light or gas bill!" I said to her as I tapped the top of her hand and laughed as I cut my eye over at her to see if she was laughing too.

"See you trying to be funny and I am serious right now."

"Okay you pray for us."

"You need to be careful. Bryce because whatever it is that is distracting you right now is causing you to lose ground spiritually."

"Are you threatening me Max'?" I asked out of curiosity because I heard a few different things that I didn't know how to take with that you need to be careful line.

"Bryce, I am your wife and I am your blood just as you are my blood and rock. We cannot operate correctly if there is something wrong with the blood."

"You're getting this from church right?"

"Bryce you know.."

"Where's my phone? I need to call the blood bank and pay our bills." I said as I cut her off before she decided to take me back to church with her second hand versions of what the shepherd told the sheep stories. Maxine would say that I perfected ducking God. I would say that I learned to cut her off precisely and I think that there is a time and place for everything.

"Your phone is right there in the door panel and it's been vibrating for the last ten minutes. As a matter of fact let me grab my phone out of my purse." she said as she tried to lean between the seats to look for her purse.

"A woman can have all the evidence in the world and still want a confession." I said under my breath as I watched her get restrained by the seatbelt from reaching into the back.

"Excuse me, what was that you said?" she asked as she was now turned forward with now her arm only reaching to the back for her purse.

"Nothing, I was just thinking out loud."

"Call Darlene." she said with one look at her cell phone without going through every social network that could possibly be downloaded to a phone first. Because whenever I have my phone in my hand all I ever hear is how much time I spend on those networks and especially while were out to dinner.

"My sister for what?" I asked as I looked over at her scrolling through her phone and back at the road.

"I don't know but I got three missed calls from her and a text saying to tell you to call her. And one missed call from your evil sister Sheryl."

"Sheryl called you?" I asked as I looked over in disbelief because my wife and Sheryl share a two word maximum relationship for over the last twenty plus years. The first two and only words to each other are hello and hello. These two have not mixed since we all were kids. Sheryl went from not liking the attention Maxine got from our sister Darlene as kids to feeling that Maxine would never be good enough for her big brother Bryce. Maxine never brushed Sheryl's loose cannon mouth to the side like everyone else has and she always tries to maintain her cool and keep her distance as much as possible.

"Yeah so you know something must be wrong if she called my phone." she replied while looking at me with her face screwed up and her lips twisted.

"Yeah something must be wrong because I have fifteen missed calls between the both of them. I will call them as soon as we get home." I said as I looked through my phone.

"Please don't do that while you are driving?" she asked as she sat her phone down on her lap.

"I'm not texting. I'm just reading." I replied as I looked down at the phone and back up at the road every few seconds.

"Same difference. You should only be driving." she said as she put her elbow onto the console and stretched her arm and hand out for me phone to give her my phone.

"I got you." I replied as I dropped my phone onto the seat between my legs and slapped her hand five.

"Thank you. Besides my phone might burn up if I dialed Sheryl's number back." she said with a laugh as she turned to look out the window.

"You two are good and funny."

"It's not me, it's her. You know that."

"It's the both of you, and I honestly think it's very entertaining."

"Darlene just texted me saying that your father got rushed to the hospital." she said as she looked at the incoming messages while adjusting the seat belt across her chest.

"Did she say why?"

"No she didn't."

"Did she say which hospital?"

"No she didn't say that either. Do you want me to call her now?"

"No I will call her once we get home. It's probably a false alarm as usual." I said as I sunk back into my seat to shake my head because we all have been through this scenario before with these hospital trips from him to get us all in one place to hear his sympathy stories.

"Well, just drop me off home so I can change and I will meet you and your sister's over there."

"I hope they didn't take him to Memorial." I said because not only do they have the worst service in the city, but that is also where they took Leah yesterday.

"No, they're not at Memorial. She just text me and said that if I am with you to tell you that they are taking him to County General and to tell you to answer your phone because Sheryl needs to be picked up."

"Okay."

"Wait, Darlene said that she needs you to pick her up from her job first before you get Sheryl because she was on her way in when she got tge call."

"Darlene is something else with that car. She could've drove to work." I replied as I just exhaled in disgust.

"If they both need to be picked up, then how did your father get to the hospital?" she asked while staring at me.

"He must've called 911. I swear I think he gets a kick out of riding in ambulances. This is the third time he has done this since last summer."

"That's no good. He shouldn't play like that." she said as she put her cell phone back into her purse and started to grab all of the napkins that she had on her lap she used to take off her make-up.

"He does it for attention." I said as I begin to turn into our driveway.

"No, no babe don't go into the drive way, let me jump out right here. I just need to get my stuff out of the back." she said while putting her hand onto my arm that was holding the steering wheel.

"Sit back, I'm pulling into the drive way because I want to go in and throw on some sweats and sneakers real quick before I go and grab them two. I'm not going to the hospital looking like this. Unless you want pick up Sheryl?" I said with a laugh as I pulled into the driveway.

"Like I said, I will meet you all down there." she said as she closed her purse with a loud thump.

"No problem. I just thought I throw that out there." I said as I unfastened my seat belt.

"Can you reach in the back and get my bible bag and those shoes for me please?"

"Got it, here you go." I said as I reached my arm to the back and grabbing her shoes off of the floor and her bible bag off of the back seat.

"I am so glad that you came with me to church this morning. Today was a special day. That was a good word." she said as she smiled and smiled while going back into her purse to take out her house keys.

"Yes. I am glad that I came today also. Max' I need to…"

"One Sunday at a time babe is…" she began to say as she unfastened the seatbelt while cutting me off.

"I was getting ready to tell you..."

"Listen to me. Look at me Bryce. What you have to do is tithe baby. You have to give back to God. He makes it possible for us to have when we don't have. I believe in it and I need you to believe in it as well." she said as she turned towards me in the seat while giving me a look of hopelessness.

"Max' listen…" I said to her as I leaned my head onto the window and rubbing my face with my left hand.

"Don't fight me on this Bryce. I saw all those tithing envelopes fall out of your bible this morning. Those are not collector's items. We have to both be on one accord or we have no chance at an abundant life."

"Max' listen I'm not about to give all my money to some preacher or to some church. I do not see where we benefit from or as you would say that we will get blessed. All I see in this world is preacher's living better than the people that they pray for." I said to her as I looked forward through the windshield at the garage door.

"The money is not for the preacher."

"So he's not on no salary and he just doing it for the Lord?"

"Bryce let me go." she said as she put her fingers into the back of each heel in one hand to pick them up and grabbing her purse and bible bag in the other.

"Oh now you want to get out because I'm talking about your church and your pastor." I said as I put the truck in park and turned the engine off.

"No I want to get out because you talking foolish."

"You know what, get out of my truck. I have to go down to this hospital and deal with this and you're starting your non-sense. Get out." I said to her as I reached over her to grab for the door latch to open the door.

"Not a problem. Your father has my prayers and you do too. Man I'm telling you, you and your punctured heart will have no closure without God." she said as she opened the door and stepped out.

"Yeah you right. Now bring some closure to my door as you get out."

Daddy Is Admitted

It was not unusual for me and Maxine to have a few good hours together and then find ourselves not speaking for the next couple of hours. I knew this tithing thing was eventually going to be an issue between us today once she saw all those envelopes. I see things one way and she sees things another way. I just don't understand why I have to give ten percent of my paycheck to a church that does not seem to be growing or does not show how it is using any of the tithe or offering money. Maxine has not once shown me where it says in the bible that I must give ten percent, but she will say that God could ask for ninety percent instead of ten. I never get an answer to any of the questions that I ask, and her escape from the conversations would always be that I couldn't pick and choose which parts of the bible I wanted to live by. Now this was even funnier to me because I always wondered how she would have sex with me every chance that we could when we first started dating, but fought me tooth and nail about how we couldn't live with each other until we were married. That to me was the ultimate pick and choose. I didn't understand how she could roll over on me the night before, but yet I couldn't stay over and wake up with her the next morning because she loved God. I always said that we all love God but we done learned a lot from Satan. As I think back I realize that maybe now we are all sexed out. We put more time into the bed than we did into our prayer life. For years we would argue that she was up to late every night reading her word when she needed to be lying down and making love to her husband. You can pray for the house all you want but you still have to take care of it. It became very quiet around the house for months as we spoke less and less. So it was no problem for me to kick her out of my car, walk in the house, and change my clothes and then leave for the hospital without saying a word. I knew it would take me a while to go get Sheryl from her apartment and Darlene from her job, so I asked them both to just catch a cab and meet me down at the hospital. I told them that I would give them their money back. It did not make sense to me for us to drive two cars and have to pay for parking them both. It seemed that my sisters were more concerned with us three all getting there at the same time instead of just them just getting there and seeing what was going on. As I got near I texted Darlene to tell her that I was looking for a parking spot close to the hospital, and that I would be right up in a few minutes.

My sister Darlene is a perfectionist. Out of all of our mother's children she is most like her in so many ways. Like Mama, Darlene is a tall, dark skinned and curvy woman that's loving, giving and into her God. She walked liked Mama, talked like Mama but couldn't cook like Mama. Nobody cooked like Mama. They both prided themselves on looking their very best at all times. Neither one of them would leave the house dressed any which way. They had to be dollied up. The only difference between the two in that area was that Darlene never went out of her way to keep up with the fashion trends or to keep her hair styled with the latest cut. Even to this day she dresses as if she's forty five, but does not look a day over thirty. My sister Sheryl always invites her out to go shopping to help her bring her style up to date but always gets shot down. Darlene still chooses to go to the same hair dresser that my mother used and first took her too and she still shops out of magazines. We all thought that she was being loyal and looking to stay connected to where Mama got her hair done and shopped, but we are now convinced that she is stuck in a different decade.

"I don't know where Bryce thinks he's going to find parking at around here. There is never anything near this hospital." Darlene said to Sheryl as they walked into an un-cleaned waiting area room that had a few visitors seated throughout on each side.

"Darlene you know that brother of yours never listens. He never did and he never will." Sheryl said as she sipped on her large cup of cold coffee as she trailed Darlene while surveying the room.

"And he's still cheap! I told him to just put that truck, jeep or whatever he wants to call it in the parking lot and that I'd pay for it. No not big brother know it all, he has to find a parking spot." Darlene said as she took off her coat and scarf and placed them on her lap as she sat down.

"Well you know your brother. He's hard headed and cheap" Sheryl said as she passed Darlene her coffee to hold so she could unbutton the jacket on her dark grey business pants suit.

"Tight and cheap at that." Darlene said as she took out her cell phone, twisted her lips and cut her eyes towards Sheryl.

"And would do anything to save himself a dollar. You know we're not seeing any cab money back right!" Sheryl said as she took her coffee back and sat down next to Darlene.

"That's your brother. He just got to do things his way. Bryce is always going to be Bryce. Sheryl I'm just praying that God can bring us through this." Darlene said as she sat back and looked around the room at the other people waiting amongst them.

"What time is it?" Sheryl asked as she sat up to sip her coffee and to look around for another clock on the wall besides the one that was behind her head.

"What is it with you Sheryl? Every time someone talks about God. You want know what time it is?" Darlene said as she threw her cell phone back into her purse and jumped forward to address Sheryl.

"Whatever. I'm just asking because that clock up there cannot be right!" Sheryl said as she pointed up behind her head to the clock.

"It is ten to." Darlene said as she slowly slid back in her seat.

"Ten to what? I just hate when people say that. It's ten to. Ten to what?" Sheryl said as she gave Darlene a long stare of disgust.

"Ten to three Sheryl relax." Darlene said as she touched Sheryl's left arm.

"Well just say 2:50 or ten minutes to three. It's ten to." Sheryl replied loudly as she swung her arm away to stop Darlene's caressing while spilling some of her coffee onto the seat.

"Well it's 2:51 now. Nine to." Darlene said with a laugh.

"Don't Darlene. Don't go there."

"Wait, wait, wait, wait. I am the big sister, so let's get that straight."

"Yeah we could see that you are the big sister. So what's your point?" Sheryl said as she looked at Darlene's hips before starting to wipe the coffee off of her wrist and the seat next to her.

My sister Sheryl would always jump at an opportunity to take a shot at Darlene about her body structure. To me Sheryl often came across as if she wanted some hips like Darlene or a chance to trade in her straight up and down figure for a different one. The same super confident in every other area Sheryl would feel slighted if someone complimented anyone else in her presence and didn't acknowledge her with at least a smile or a look.

Sheryl perfected using Darlene's sensitivity to her advantage and to keep Darlene under her thumb as much as she could. Sheryl learned early how to beat Darlene down mentally and also how to massage her back to happiness.

"Look Sheryl, I don't have it in me today. So you and nasty little attitude need to take a break for at least one day."

"Yeah okay."

"What time is Baby Boy getting in?" Darlene asked as she passed Sheryl some napkins out of her purse.

"I have no idea." Sheryl said as she wiped down her cup and looked around for the closest trashcan to throw the napkins into.

"Well Aunt Vye's train pulls in around four or five I believe, I'm not sure."

"You must be going home to get your car and to get her because you know she cannot ride in my car." Sheryl lashed out while wrapping the last good napkin around her cup.

"Come on Sheryl you need to stop all that. Aunt Vye and Mom had their differences, not you and Aunt Vye. Can we just get together and conduct ourselves like a family for once. Why do we have to make things so hard?" Darlene asked as she sat up to rub Sheryl on her shoulder.

"I guess we can try." Sheryl said as she moved her feet over to let the janitor sweep the floor while tossing the napkins into his trash can.

"Thank you Sheryl."

"But she is still going to have to ride in your car and stay over at your house, because she will not set a foot into my apartment."

"That is alright with me. Because Sheryl, I am too blessed to be stressed." Darlene said as she rocked back in her seat and tapped both feet on the floor about five times each.

"And oh yeah, she has got to go to church with you. Because she is not and I repeat not, going to embarrass me at my church! Carrying on like she crazy." Sheryl said as her forehead got smaller and smaller with every word.

"Well you know Aunt Vye. She comes in with a praise, shouting from the door." Darlene said as she started to shake again in excitement.

"With her big ole' upper body and little people legs. Poor lady shaped like a wisdom tooth. And got the nerve to think she sexy, she better go somewhere and sit down, carrying on with that foolishness." Sheryl said while trying to hold back her laughter.

"Sheryl you need help." Darlene said as she cried and laughed so hard that she had to press her hand up against her chest as she coughed to catch her breath.

"You've seen her body. Tell me she not shaped like a wisdom tooth? Tell me Darlene. Tell me." Sheryl asked as she laughed and patted Darlene on her back.

"Sheryl I'm not going there with you." Darlene said as she coughed, laughed and wiped away the tears.

"Because you know I'm telling the truth." Sheryl said as she sat back in the seat with her legs crossed to finish sipping on her coffee while grinning from ear to ear.

"Look can we just enjoy one another like Mom would want us to? Doesn't it feel like old times when we get together little sis'?" Darlene coughed out as she patted on Sheryl's knee with one hand and squeezed on her hat and scarf in the other.

"It sure does. But I hope it's with less arguing. Do you remember the last time we all got together for Mom's funeral and I almost had to slap cousin!

What is her name again?" Sheryl asked as she tapped her foot while looking around the room for the name to come to her.

"Who?"

"You know the one with the buck teeth and the bad weave." Sheryl said as she continued to get excited by slapping her knee and pulling on Darlene's arm.

"Cousin Candy?" Darlene asked.

"Yes girl. Why she just thought that she could come up in my Mama's house and just have all of her jewelry," Sheryl said as she stood up and got into a fighting stance in front of Darlene.

"You know you stupid right." Darlene said as she covered her mouth with her scarf to muffle her cough.

"Darlene you know I almost wrapped that weave around her neck about two or three times before Bryce pulled me up off of her!" Sheryl said as she backed up a few steps and started to swing one of her arms in a circular motion.

"You know you touched right? And need I say not by an angel. I tell you this though. I sure do miss Mama and that house. It is amazing how everything still looks exactly the same."

"Yes it does. The dining room set is still in good condition after all of these years. Do you remember that sofa set and that plastic that Mama kept on it to try and make it last forever?"

"Yes Lord I remember the plastic on that couch and the back of my legs remembers that plastic too." Darlene said as she shook her head and rubbed the back of her leg to see if the scars from their childhood were still there.

"Don't you miss our room?" Sheryl asked as she looked in a daze in the direction of a family of four that was sitting and talking on the other side of the room.

"Yes I do Sis'. I remember Bryce and Baby Boy on one side of the room. You and me on our side."

"Two big ole' headed boys splitting one bed. I just remember they're side being such a mess." Sheryl said as she turned to look at Darlene.

"We had a bed full of dolls and that comforter slash quilt that Mama made." Darlene said as she smiled and looked up at the ceiling.

"I remember it like it was yesterday."

"Yeah and you know to this day that your brothers still deny that they ever played with cabbage patch dolls." Darlene said as she laughed and scratched her arm.

"I know they didn't. I know that Joseph King Jr. of all people didn't say that. Because he was the main one, I just knew that he was going to grow up and be a hair stylist or something." Sheryl said as she put her coffee cup between her legs and sat up to take off her suit jacket.

"Yes he did. But you know what Sheryl, I have the pictures. I have the Polaroid's to prove it."

"I remember Mama and her camera and how she used to sit us down. You broke that camera too." Sheryl said as they both sat back.

"Girls, girls. Sheryl, Darlene." They hear in Mama's voice as they pop up in their seats to pay attention.

"Yes Mama?" They replied.

"Did y'all make up them beds and finish those dishes like I asked y'all too?" Mama would ask as she sat in her favorite night gown, in her favorite love seat while folding over five loads of clothes and having the dinner cooking in the oven at the same time.

"Yes Mama, yes we did."

"Sheryl."

"Yes Mama?" Sheryl replied as she sat up straight with her hands folded on her lap.

"Did you do your hair like I told you?"

"Yes Mama and I did it up just like you told me. Bang in the front, part in the middle with two pigtails." Sheryl said as she touched every part of her head that Mama asked about to show her.

"That's Mama's baby. Now Darlene."

"Yes Mama?" Darlene replied as he jumped up to her feet with excitement.

"Go upstairs and run some bathwater for you and your sister. I want y'all to get yourselves ready for church. You know Mama don't like to be late for worship." Mama would say with such authority because she did not play when it came time for us to be at church. Mama believed that you started preparing for Sunday morning service on Saturday night. She lived by the motto of to be on time is to be late.

"Yes Mama." Darlene said as she nodded her head to agree before sitting down.

"I miss Mama so much." Sheryl said as she put her clenched hands under her nose and over her mouth.

"Mama use to always say that she had two young ladies that she only had to tell things to once. But when she talked to me about Bryce, she would tell me "Darlene I need you to pray for your brother because he needs some work.""

"I never heard words more true." Sheryl said.

"Sheryl I remember Mama telling me the story of how she sent Bryce to the store one day for some groceries and she said she told him to watch the light as he crossed the street and to wait for it to turn green before he crossed. You know what this boy told Mama?"

"What?" Sheryl asked as she looked at Darlene with curiosity.

"Bryce said Mama. Ain't no light ever in the history of crossing the street has never, ever hit anybody. I gotta' look out for them cars."

"No he didn't."

"Sheryl I tell you I am not lying. All Mama could say to me after I stopped laughing was, Pray for my child, pray for your brother." Darlene said as she laughed while picking up her hat and scarf off of the floor.

I sure am hungry like a hostage and these vending machines are the worst. These broke machines keep taken my money. Didn't this hospital used to have a cafe? What happened to this place?" Bryce said as he walked into the waiting area room with a bottle of Sprite soda and a pack of Twizzlers.

"Speaking of the devil." Sheryl said to Darlene as she took the last sip of her coffee.

"Mr. Cheap." Darlene said as she elbowed Sheryl.

"Every other minute you talking about getting something to eat or you sick.

What's up Bryce? Is your wife pregnant or something? Come on Big Bro'; you could talk to me!" Sheryl said as she held up her cup in front of her mouth.

"Don't you start Sheryl! You know my wife cannot have kids and besides we're separated right now." Bryce said as he sat down across from Sheryl and Darlene while giving them both the nastiest look that he could come up with.

"Separated?" Darlene asked as she widened her eyes.

"Yes Darlene. Separated like divide. What part don't you understand?"

"Excuse me!" Darlene asked as she sat up.

"Makes you wonder why." Sheryl said as she stood up to walk to the trash can to throw her cup away.

"Look now is not the time to discuss my life! Besides Sheryl, you chose to chase relationships with a lot of people. Mostly women I do remember. Instead of chasing for a relationship with God, so don't get me started on you!" Bryce barked as he watched Sheryl walk to the trash can.

"Yes I did Bryce King. But I am delivered from all of that. And I am deeply rooted within' the church now. Can you say the same thing? Can you?" Sheryl said as she stared Bryce down while walking back to sit in her seat.

"Oh you deeply rooted now?" Bryce said as he pointed his finger and cut his eyes at Sheryl.

"She right Bryce, because some of us is in the church, but the church is not in us!"

"Darlene you need to stop. Because I don't see anyone following you to church! You stay calling for someone to pick you up. Gas is not that high. God has blessed both of you with a car and who do either one of you pick up to take with you to church? No one!"

"All he will ever see is what other people do wrong Darlene."

"You two will shout with someone at eleven and then drive by them at the bus stop by one thirty."

"My car not good on gas and it's a coupe, and we not even out by one thirty, so you can't be talking to me!" Darlene said as she sat back to cross her legs and fold her arms.

"All that booty and you get a coupe." Bryce said as he looked at Darlene.

"You got some nerve." Sheryl said as she sat up.

"Anyway. How did they say he was doing?" Bryce asked as he waved off Sheryl's menacing look with his hand.

"How is our father doing you mean?" Sheryl asked as she inched up closer to the edge of the seat.

"Please not right now with this who is he to you stuff. Look Bryce we were waiting for you before we went in." Darlene said as she sat back in her seat.

"Your father is going to be real happy to see you Bryce." Sheryl said as she smiled at Bryce.

"Yes. It really is going to make his heart glad to see you. He loves him some Bryce." Darlene said as she stood up to walk over to a sitting Bryce with her arms outstretched to hug him.

"I don't know why. Listen I'm only here because you two insisted. Some things, issues and people, you just need to let go away. I've washed my hands with this man." Bryce said as he looked up at Darlene standing over him with her arms now draped to her side.

"Go away? You've washed your hands? Bryce King this is your father we're talking about." Sheryl said as she jumped to her feet and walked over to Bryce and Darlene.

"Yes it is and don't remind me." Bryce grunted as he looked up at Sheryl.

"You haven't changed one bit. You still that same self-centered fool." Sheryl screamed as she kneed Bryce in his leg before turning and walking back to her seat.

"Self-centered?" Bryce screamed as he shoved Darlene to the side so that he could walk after Sheryl.

"Yes I said it, self-centered!" Sheryl replied as she looked up at Bryce as they stood face to chest.

"Look. However you want to cut it Bryce. He is still your father. He brought you into this world..." Darlene said as she grabbed Bryce by his arm to turn him around to face her.

"Yes he did bring me into this world, but what else has he done for me since then? Has he shown me how to be a man? I had to learn to live this life for myself and by myself!" Bryce said as he grinded his teeth while looking directly into Darlene's face.

"You killing me right now!" Sheryl said as she sat down, twisted her lips and pointed her finger at Bryce.

"This man spent the first years of our lives teaching us how to walk and talk, and then spent the rest of our childhood telling us to shut up and sit down." Bryce said as he stood over Sheryl while patting the back of his right hand into his left palm.

"You are really killing me right now." Sheryl said to Bryce as Darlene started to walk off.

"And you know what Darlene, every man should have some type of plan for his family." Bryce said to Sheryl in a nasty tone before he turned around to walk behind a pacing Darlene.

"You need to grow up at some point." Sheryl said.

"What was Dad's plan? Did he love you despite your drinking habit Darlene? Did he? Yeah, yeah y'all real quiet now. Oh please don't sit on the Amen's now." Bryce said as he walked up behind Darlene to talk to the back of her head as she covered her face with her hand.

"Daddy was in a whole lot of pain back then." Darlene said as she turned around to face Bryce.

"Come on y'all. Am I the only one who seen him beat on Mom? Am I? This man use to try and smack the brightness out of her eyes." Bryce screamed as he stared at Darlene before turning to look at Sheryl.

"Bryce we were kids." Darlene blurted as she started to cry while moving out of the way of a couple rushing to leave out of the room.

"And we all stood around helpless!" Bryce said as he threw himself down into a seat.

"No you are not the only one Bryce. But how long are you going to hold this against Dad?" Sheryl asked as she sat up.

"Possibly forever. Possibly until and long after that man is gone." Bryce said as he laid his head back against the wall while looking up at the ceiling.

"I can't believe I'm hearing this. I really can't believe that I'm hearing this! Mama taught us to pray for one another. I mean we prayed for Mama, we prayed for Dad and I'm praying for you too Bryce." Darlene said as she tried to hold back tears and walked towards the doorway.

"Mom would be so disappointed with you right now." Sheryl said as she looked Bryce up and down as she passed him to head to Darlene.

"Dad tore this family apart. Look I don't know what type of affect his beating on Mom had on you two, but I despise him for it. Fool chasing her through the house, beating on her! He can't beat on her now." Bryce said as he rocked back and forth while looking at the floor and then towards Sheryl and Darlene.

"Bryce stop." Darlene screamed as she walked back towards Bryce while wiping away her tears with the back of her hand.

"Stop is exactly what we had to scream and whisper our entire childhood. I'll never forget those days of us all crying and him yelling at Mama." Bryce said as he smacked down his bottle of soda off of the seat next to him.

"Josephine! Josephine! Come here woman. Don't make me come up them stairs. You know I'll do it!" Dad screamed. "Josephine! You spend more time down at that church, than you spend at home with your own husband and I'm tired of it. I said I am tired of it. Now don't make me come lay hands on you. Ain't that how y'all like it down at the church?" Dad said as he laughed and rubbed his hands together with his vodka bottle under his armpit. "And you got the nerve to make some food for that church on the stove that I paid for. Cook another pan of chicken if you want and try to walk it up outta' here. See what happen. Wit' ya' do not touch this, it's for the pastor note. And while you hiding and praying, you better pray that I don't get hungry! Because that chicken gon' get ate and a few of them pieces might just arrive at that church with some bite marks in them. Ooh you so lucky I'm too tired to come up these stairs. And you know what, as a matter of fact I want everybody to get up, children too. Everybody up, because I'm up. I know y'all listening, because I heard the door crack open. But I'm still gonna' say it twice so I don't have to repeat myself and I'm also going to say it slow, so that I could be understood. So you kids put some feet on the floor now! Come on Josey, come on baby, I just wanna' talk. I just wanna' talk to you, I'm sorry baby. You know it will all be okay in the morning. Darlene stop, all that crying, I can't even hear myself think." Dad said as he stumbled down the hallway to the living room to fall onto the couch.

"There were times when Mama couldn't even come to open school night for us because she was all black, blue and embarrassed." Bryce said as he stood up to walk around.

"The bible says we must learn to forgive." Darlene said as she walked backed to her seat with her eyes colored red from crying and rubbing.

"Old drunken mad man. Drinking all that drink Blockinfall." Bryce said as he walked to the doorway to look up and down the hallway.

"Bryce What is Blockinfall?" Sheryl asked as she sat next to Darlene to comfort her.

"It's liquor. It's when you walk up a block and you fall." Bryce said as he stumbled back towards Sheryl and Darlene in a drunken fashion.

"Bryce you're not funny." Darlene said as she sat up.

"I would catch him bragging, laughing and joking with his friends. I'd hear him say, you know what they say about a woman with two black eyes right?"

"No what do they say?" Sheryl asked.

"He would say that's someone that you had to tell the same thing to twice." Bryce said as he threw shadow punches into the air.

"Do you read the bible son?" a homeless looking lady asked from across the room.

"Excuse me?" Bryce replied.

"I asked you if you read the bible Sir. Because the bible says that we should Get along with each other and forgive each other. If someone does wrong to you, forgive that person because the Lord forgave you, it's in Colossians 3:13." the Homeless Lady asked in a southern drawl as she shifted her belongings around on the chair next to her and near her feet.

"Look lady, all I can say right now, is that time heals all wounds." Bryce replied as he looked over and beyond the Homeless Lady.

"Yes it does. But we're in a hospital right now, and from listening to you and your sisters, your family was a close knit one. That man in that room as you call him is your Daddy and you should love him, forgive him. Your family needs togetherness more than ever right now young man" said the Homeless Lady as she pointed to the doorway while walking closer to Bryce.

"Miss I don't think that you're in any position to tell anyone how to live their life. You look homeless." Bryce said as he took a step back to look her up and down.

"Bryce!" Darlene yelled.

"No. Who does she think she is?" Bryce replied without once taking his eyes off the Homeless Lady.

"No it's okay Darlene. Darlene it is right?" The Homeless Lady asked as she twirled a brown towel and circled around Bryce.

"Yes it's Darlene." Darlene replied as she watched the Homeless Lady and Bryce's every move.

"Cool, nice to meet you. But it's okay Darlene because he has the right to his opinion. You see I serve an on time God who can change things around in less than a second. My God has me right where he needs me, so I'm going to praise him in season and out of season." The Homeless Lady said as she backed up and danced.

"I know that's right." Darlene said as she wiped her eyes.

"Are we about to have church right here?" Bryce asked as he opened his arms and looked over at Sheryl and Darlene.

"Exactly." Sheryl said as she shifted to sit sideways in her seat while folding her arms.

"You know my father whom I love very deeply use to tell me all the time, that it's one thing to love God when your let it, but it's a whole nother' thing to love him when your shut out." The Homeless Lady said as she laid her brown towel on the floor before squatting down to get into a praying position.

"Well you definitely look like your shut out." Bryce said in laughter as he looked over at a laughing Sheryl.

"Bryce!" Darlene yelled.

"It's alright Darlene. You did say it was Darlene right?" The Homeless Lady said as she stood up to dust off her shirt and pants before walking up over to Bryce.

"Yes it's Darlene. Why you keep asking me if I'm me?" Darlene replied.

"Well it's alright Darlene, because they don't come so big that God can't break them down. And though he may slay me today, I still trust in him. And yes I do need change, but I will not change my faith in God because things are not like or what I would want them to be." The Homeless Lady said as she combed her hair to the back with one hand and smoothed it down with the other. She then put the comb in the back of her hair as she pulled out an old ripped up bible with no cover and the pages hanging loose out of her back pants pocket to hold up.

"So you have all the answers too? Okay I'm done now. We have an educated homeless person." Bryce said as he started to look into all of his pockets for his truck keys.

"Look folk, I'm just trying to make you aware that time can run out while you are letting your wounds heal. You have to learn to forgive, and to throw all that hurt into the sea of forgetfulness. Young man life is too short to be walking around with all that hurt in your heart. Let it go. That is a nice a sweater. Is that from the flea market on third because I got it in blue?" The Homeless Lady asked as she circled around Bryce before touching his sweater.

"Okay now I've heard enough. I'm going to go and find me something to eat and to burn this sweater. You two can stay here with Ms. Info." Bryce said as he stepped back away from the Homeless Lady while throwing his keys up in the air to catch them before turning to walk out.

"Uhhm' we need to go in and see about Daddy. Where do you think you going?" Sheryl asked as she stood up in the aisle and put her hand into Bryce's chest to block him from walking out.

"Bryce, what the lady is trying to tell you is right." Darlene said as she walked over to him and Sheryl.

"Better yet. I think I'm gonna' go to the train station to pick up Aunt Vye, I'll see y'all in a minute." Bryce said as he nudged Sheryl out of his way to walk out.

"Bryce that is your problem right there! You walk around like no one can't tell you anything!" Sheryl screamed as she walked behind him while trying to grab him by the sweater.

"Sheryl please!" Bryce said as he continued to walk out while waiving Sheryl off with his hand.

"No you please. Because you will never know whose hands God will put you into if you were to ever fall ill." Sheryl said to the back of Bryce's head as he walked out without looking back at her.

"I am so sorry miss? Can you please accept my apologies for my brother? He just needs a little prayer." Darlene said to the Homeless Lady as she walked over to the other side of the room to go sit next to her.

"It's okay sweetie. It's obvious that your brother is in a lot of pain or has some very stressful things on his mind. But don't y'all worry, because God will do his work with your brother and for your father. I believe that."

"I receive that." Darlene replied.

"Darlene come on we need to go and see how Dad is doing." Sheryl said as she grabbed Darlene's coat and scarf.

"Okay Sheryl. Miss I appreciate your kind words and trust me, I receive them all."

"Darlene." Sheryl called out as she huffed and puffed with her hand on her hips.

"Miss you take care now." Darlene said as she patted the Homeless Lady on her knee while trying to pass her twenty dollars inside of her closed hand as she got up.

"You take care as well. I'll be right here. I don't have anywhere to go. I lost my family, I lost everything. I lost my husband, my home and my job. Lost everything I had.

All washed away right from up under my feet. All I have is God." The Homeless Lady said as she leaned forward onto her shopping cart to press down on the black bags that she had sitting on the top.

"Well sister if all you have left is God, than you will be okay." Darlene said as she was now being pulled away by her arm by Sheryl.

"Oh I can testify to that, because Hurricane Katrina changed my life." said the Homeless Lady as she grimaced and slowly sat back as if her back was now hurting.

"Hurricane Katrna? That's terrible." Darlene asked as she walked back over to sit down next to the Homeless Lady.

"Look I am so sorry to hear all of this but we have to go." Sheryl said as she walked back over to give the Homeless Lady a nasty look and to place Darlene's hat and scarf on her lap.

"Sheryl I'm coming. My friend I need you to keep your head up because God will do it for you. I know he will." Darlene said as she looked up at Sheryl before turning her attention to rub the Homeless Lady's shoulder.

"Oh so now y'all friends and now you gon' actually start prophalying to her too huh?" Sheryl said as she shook her head, took out her hand sanitizer to pour some into her hands and walk off.

"How do you roll with that devil?" The Homeless Lady whispered as she leaned into Darlene.

"I heard that." Sheryl said before she could get to the doorway.

"Miss that is my sister and she is not the devil. I'm praying for her and I am praying for you too."

"I pray that you hurry up Darlene." Sheryl said as she stood in the middle of the room rubbing in the hand sanitizer.

"I thank you Darlene, but she's the one who needs the prayers." The Homeless Lady said as she leaned forward to look at Sheryl.

"Excuse me?" Sheryl said as she started to walk back hard towards Darlene and the Homeless Lady.

"Let's go." Darlene said as she stood up to stop Sheryl before she got to close.

Oh because I know that she's not talking to me." Sheryl said as she talked around Darlene who was push-ing her back.

"Yeah and you deeply rooted in the church I see. But let me tell you this sister, the doors of this church over here are now open. What you wanna' do? Will there be one? I said will there be one?" The Homeless Lady as she stood up to move her shopping cart and rolled up her shirt sleeves.

"There will not be any fighting today. Sheryl I'm going to need you to walk that way and miss I'm going to need you to take it easy and bring it down a little bit. Because you two are not about to do this. Not here and not now." Darlene said as she turned Sheryl around to push her out of the room.

"Yes you right. I'm so sorry. You two ladies go on back there and check on your Daddy. I know he will pull through. I know he is going to make it. Go on now Darlene. Go on now and catch up to ya' sister. And make sure when you catch up to her, tell her that she's also walking the wrong way, because your Daddy's room is that way. Trust me I know everybody and I know the building."

The Results

I had heard enough in that hospital. I wasn't even there for twenty minutes and they started with their nonsense. I needed to get in my car and drive as far away from that hospital I can. My phone had seven missed calls from my wife to my Aunt Vye who were both calling me to remind me about Aunt Vye needing to be picked up at the bus station. I assumed the unknown and private numbers that called me were from either Leah's family or the police, and I wasn't about to call them back until I cooled off or had my story together. I'm embarrassed to say that after two years of an affair with Leah the only thing that I really knew about her was her first name, last name and her cell phone number. She almost died during the abortion all because she used her girlfriend's insurance card to avoid paying for the procedure even after I gave her the money to cover it. The doctor' went by the medical records on file and based the anesthia dosage off of that. With Leah's girlfriend having a heart condition that changed how Leah was treated as a patient. I spent almost two hours of explaining my relationship to her to the police. We went through her phone and pocketbook looking for some family members or anyone that we could contact. Of course I knew none of her family members or any of her friends because we never talked about them. All we ever did was meet up and have sex. No restaurants, no movies, no walks in the park, it was strictly sex. We were both okay with this arrangement. Wrong and all, Leah was everything I needed for those moments that we spent together. She had a great personality, no kids and was there whenever I needed her. We would get together at least three times a month and now I don't even know where to start to tell someone who she really loves that she is laid up in a hospital in stable condition. I had to leave all of my contact information with the police officers that took the report at the clinic. Using her girlfriend's coverage and identification made the situation worst. I didn't know if I should contact a lawyer to cover me or if I should just abandon the situation and throw it all on her. My best bet was to just start thinking of what I was going to say to Maxine if she found out. I knew I needed to call her and apologize to her for kicking her out of the truck, but she probably would just go on a rant as usual about of all the things that I don't do. So I guess that apology can wait and I will just text her to listen out for Baby Boy and update her on what's going on at the hospital. As I lifted my cell phone off my lap, I let the car roll to the red light. A text from Max' came through letting me know that she left me a voicemail saying that she grabbed Baby Boy and they were on the way to the house. With Maxine picking up Baby Boy that allowed me to go straight to the bus station to pick up Aunt Vye, which was only about five to ten minutes from where I was. Now my Aunt Vye is cut from a different cloth and I knew that I would be in for some good and long lecturing whether it was concerning me or not. But this is who my aunt was and either you loved her or you didn't. She will tell you in a minute that she is Joseph King Sr.'s baby sister and that she don't take no junk off of nobody and that she loves the Lord with all her heart within the same breath. I could never figure it out, so I just gave up trying to and I loved her for who she was at that moment. Now, how my other siblings feel about her was another story. My sister Darlene has great patience with Aunt Vye and I believe it comes from the ten plus years that she served in the Navy. One of my sister's greatest accomplishments in her Navy career was her making Sargent. She was definitely a soldier in my eyes and took everything like a champ, but she also allowed herself to suffer in silence along the way. She missed out on having a family because she wanted to dedicate her life to her career in the service, and that decision ultimately lead to the end of the little bit of happiness that was left in her marriage. Her husband gave her the choice of either it was going to be him or the Navy. He wanted to start a family and have a few children and she didn't. I believed that she loved him, but she just loved the Navy more. Now my sister Sheryl was a whole different story. She was a rebellious child. She looked more like Mama in the face than any of us but had Dad's slim built. Sheryl had the flattest butt but walked around like she had the best shape ever made. She was not short on confidence. She gave our mother a hard time over everything, and she definitely did not have any respect for Aunt Vye as a child and she doesn't respect her to this day. If those two were left in a room together, I would say let us pray for the room. My Aunt is very outspoken just like Sheryl and my aunt would play on one of Sheryl's most noticeable traits. Sheryl was a tom boy growing up and didn't go out of her way to disguise that she was more attracted to girls than boys. She would always tell me that she wish that she was born a boy and that God messed up. This theory of hers caused a great wedge in our family once it came out from Sheryl during one of her rants around the house. I would always be there for her to talk to because it became clear very early that I was the only one who would listen to her. I loved my sister regardless of who she decided to lay down with. She respected my view that God loves the sinner but not the sin and we were cool. I would only throw it at her in an argument to get her riled up. Sheryl always felt misunderstood within our family and irritated her even more when Aunt Vye would call her a confused soul. My Aunt's words about Sheryl fueled the hate between her, my mother and my Aunt. It didn't sit well with my mother that her sister in law would call her own niece a confused soul, but what also burnt my mother was that Aunt Vye would harass Sheryl about her wishes to have been born a boy. The usual argument started whenever Aunt Vye was around and asked my mother" If God is perfect and you teaching your kids that, then "How can one of your kids feel that God messed up?" This was always a guaranteed fire starter. She would have my mother trapped but there was still no messing with her kids. I always believed that the issue of Sheryl displaying her feelings around the house played a role into Baby Boy being so secluded. He was always a quiet kid and he always felt like he was an accident. I guess us calling him an "Oops Baby" didn't help much either. He was seventeen years younger than me and ten years younger than Sheryl, who was the baby for so many years. I think we all treated him unfairly at some point because we either had to take him with us everywhere we went, and if we didn't then we couldn't go. And if it wasn't that, then it was like we were his baby sitters or got forced to play with him. Looking back I could see how we took out our frustrations on him for no reasons and also how we showed our jealousy towards him for Mama treating him like the baby he was. It was great to see out little brother finally grow to be almost six feet tall because he had this height issue it seemed since he came out of the womb. We disconnected ourselves as his brother and sisters once Mama died and we failed to offer him any guidance or opinions on what college to attend. We just let him go to the world. Which I guess made it easy for us to adapt to the distance of him being away in school on the west coast by himself.

"Max' we sure are glad that you were home when we called, because I don't have anyone's new cell phone number." Baby Boy said as he pulled two suitcases into the house while trying to adjust his shoulder bag.

"Don't worry Baby Boy it's not a problem. We are family and family is supposed to be there for each other." Maxine said while grabbing Baby Boy's garment bag from over his arm.

"Well I want to say thank you as well Maxine. You are a life saver, because that airport terminal was stinking and I know we would've been sitting there for hours and hours if you wouldn't have come to the rescue." said Baby Boy's girlfriend Denise as she pulled her suitcase along.

"Max' you know me and my baby are looking to follow in you and Bryce's footsteps. We've decided that we are going to tie that knot, have some kids and enjoy this life together." he said as he walked over and hugged Denise.

"Oh is that right?" Maxine asked.

"That's right baby. Maxine I have heard so many great things about you and Bryce."

"Oh you have young lady?"

"This boy here, he looks up to his big brother so much, and not to mention that I've been watching you on them soap operas that you star in. What is it called "Mama I Burned the Fish Grease"? Maxine you are doing your thing." Denise said as she put her Louis Vuitton duffel bag down on the love seat before walking over to Maxine.

"Why thank you Denise, but it's called "Mama I Turned A New Leaf". And those are repeats. But Denise let me tell you something. Marriage and life is what you make it. You can make it peaceful and wonderful with someone, or you can make it peaceful and wonderful all by yourself." Maxine said to Denise as she pulled her into her.

"Well don't worry honey. We are going to make it peaceful and wonderful together. And I see you still can't whisper huh Max'." Baby Boy said from the couch on the other side of the room as he looked through his suitcase.

"Haha' very funny young man." Maxine said as she picked up a pair of Bryce's sneakers.

"That's right baby, peaceful and wonderful together." Denise said as she strutted over to kiss him.

"Look at you two all googly eyed!"

"I'm all googly eyed because I have to use the little ladies room. Which way is it Max'?" Denise asked as she turned around to Maxine.

"I can show you where it's at baby." Baby Boy said as he ran up behind her to kiss her on the neck.

"No you will not show her. Denise you are crazy. I like you already. The little ladies room is right this way. Leave them bags and Joseph right there and you come with me."

"Be right back baby."

"Hurry, hurry sugar." Baby Boy said as he moved all of the suitcases and bags to the corner of the room.

"Hey, hey. You two are going to have to cut all of this baby, baby, sugar sugar stuff ."

"Okay. Okay. I see you soon honey bunch." Denise said as she blew Baby Boy two kisses before exiting.

"Girl come on, he is not going nowhere." Maxine said as she grabbed Denise's arm.

"Look at the pictures. Look at this house. Man I miss this house. The sweet smell of Mama's cooking in the air. All of us upstairs either playing or fighting. Man I miss this house. I can still hear us arguing over the cake bowl now. Who's getting the spoon? Who's getting the mixer sticks? We would misdial on the rotary phone. Oops, stuck your finger into the wrong number, gotta' start dialing all over again. With Dad out running the streets. Dad out running the streets." Baby Boy said to himself as he walked around the living room reminiscing before he dropped down on the couch.

"Joseph." He hears in Mama's voice as he starts to look around the room for her.

"Yes Mama?" he replied as he slowly sat back in disappointment from not seeing Mama.

"Pick your head up boy!"

"But Mama I just got cut from the junior high school basketball team tryouts. They said I wasn't good enough. They said I wasn't tall enough." He said as he sulked and sunk into the couch.

"Baby Boy don't you worry about that. Don't you study today's failures. You pick yourself up and you come back better and stronger for tomorrow. Do you hear me Joseph King Jr.? Do you hear your mother talking to you?"

"Yes Mama I hear you. I'll be better next time Mama. I promise I will." he replied as he sat up and grabbed Mama's picture off of the glass table that was in front of him.

"Now you pull it together and you make Mama proud. Because it's not always a failure, sometimes it's just an experience that you just have to go through Joseph. Do you hear me?"

"Yes Mama." he said as he ran his fingers across and around the wooden picture frame that somehow stayed in perfect shape over the water stained picture under the glass.

"Now I don't want to see no more pouting, and I definitely don't want to see your head hung low. So now go on outside and practice, play, do something."

"Mama you should see me now. I've gotten taller. I'm the star of my college basketball team. Mama I'm doing so well. Mama, don't go. Mama." he said as he stood up with the picture in his hand to walk towards the dining room doorway where he thought he heard Mama's voice coming from..

"Is that my college star nephew?" Aunt Vye said as she stood in the hallway from the opposite side of the room with her suitcase in one hand and a collection full of other bags in her other hand.

"Aunt Vye!" Baby Boy shouted as he lifted his head up while wiping away his tears.

"Hey baby, come on over here and give yo' Aunt Vye a big hug."

"I miss you so much Auntie." he said as he looked around for Mama one last time and sitting her picture down on the end table before walking over to Aunt Vye.

"I miss you too baby, but are you gon' grab some of these bags out of my hands?"

"Oh I'm sorry Auntie, let me grab that big bag." he said as he reached to get everything out of her hand.

"Oh no not this one sugar. Auntie may have to get at you if you touch her goodie bag." she replied as she dipped back to avoid Baby Boy from grabbing the big bag while hitting him in his knee with her suitcase.

"Oh my bad."

"Look it here, look it here. If it's not my little brother Jojo, the Baby Boy." Bryce said as he walked in with the remainder of Aunt Vye's bags of food from traveling.

"Big bro' what's good? Baby Boy asked as he walked towards Bryce with Aunt Vye's suitcase.

"It's good to see you. That's what's good! You look good kid. You know I could never get a good look at you on television as you move with that basketball." Bryce said as he hugged him the best he could with all of Aunt Vye's bags still in his hands.

It was good to finally see my little brother Jojo, the Baby Boy. He was now all grown up and coming into his own. We all thought for a while that he would eventually grow up and be gay because he possessed way too many female tendencies to us. He would do all of the doll babies hair better than Darlene and Sheryl, he was super clingy to Mama and we all agreed that he was too in touch with his feelings. These were some of the things we witnessed and labeled him with as his siblings. We were wrong all along. Baby Boy just happened to be a more well-rounded individual than anyone of us were. He studied hard in school, got great grade and never got himself into any trouble, while the three of us struggled in school with our school work and behavior before eventually pulling it together. I never put my brother under my wing like I should have because I felt he got good guidance from Dad and anything that I could offer would be irrelevant. To this day I don't understand how he was named a junior and I wasn't. But I'm glad today to see his growth.

"I'm trying to get better every year Big bro'.".

"You know you still running fast as if you are still getting chased home from school by them female bullies. You know they never could catch you." Bryce said as he sat the bags on the living room table.

"You funny man, but Bryce it's not me. All the credit goes to God, he did it." Baby Boy said as he sat Aunt Vye's suitcase down next to his luggage.

"Amen Joseph." Aunt Vye said.

"I thank the Lord every day for him waking me up and giving me the strength to praise him and to play college basketball."

"Praise the lord Joseph you know you talking right" Aunt Vye said as she grabbed the back of the love seat and started to dance.

"Aunt Vye that's enough." Bryce and Baby Boy said together.

"Hey Aunt Vye. Hey Bryce." Maxine said as she walked into the room with a oven mitten on one hand.

"Hey Max'." Bryce lowly said under his breath.

"So how you keeping up Ms. Alabama? I see you still looking as beautiful as you did ten years ago!" Aunt Vye said as she walked towards Maxine with her arms outstretched.

"Thank you Aunt Vye. I'm trying." Maxine said as she met her halfway to hug her.

"You welcome sugar and you know you don't have to try too hard with yo' beautiful self. How's my nephew treating you?" Aunt Vye said as she looked Maxine over.

"So what would you guys like to eat for dinner tonight? I think I'm going to cook. I was thinking about some fried turkey with some extra stuffing and some collard greens." Maxine said as she waived the mitten and looked around at everyone except Aunt Vye.

"I guess he's not treating you too well. Because the minute somebody asked me about Buford, my second husband. The first thing I brought up we're some collard greens. Bless his soul, and I sure could go for some greens right about now. Did you say you smoked turkey?" Aunt Vye said as she slowly sat down in the love seat while shaking her head.

"Uhmm Aunt Vye, let me get you over to this hospital so that you can see your brother." Bryce said as he walked over to Aunt Vye.

"What's up Bryce? Oh you don't know how to treat a lady all of a sudden? Boy I'm talking to you! Don't you make me throw one of these expensive fifteen dollar shoes at you!" Aunt Vye said as she kicked her leg at Bryce as he walked up to her.

"Auntie it looks like we will be here waiting all night on an answer. Let's go." Baby Boy said as he took a seat.

"Bryce, that is a good woman right there."

"Right where?" Bryce asked Aunt Vye.

"Boy don't you get stupid." Aunt Vye screamed out.

"Get?" Maxine mumbled.

"Maxine is a good woman, don't you go and mess up a good thing! Now, I'm gon' say this as nice as I can to you Bryce. God cannot get rid of your nasty attitude, if you are not ready to let go of it yourself. Oh, see you got me preaching now." Aunt Vye said as she started to shake in the seat with her arms spread open in the air.

"Let him use ya'!" Baby Boy said as he got up to walk to the hallway.

"I'm coming Baby Boy, just give me one second." Aunt Vye said as she fanned herself and checked into her bra for her small change purse.

"Take ya' time Auntie." Baby Boy said from the hallway as he looked his and Bryce's old trophies that lined the wall.

"Whoo, you kids now a days don't know how to sit down at all, at least for a few seconds. Cause' Lord knows that I am tired in my spirit and in my soul. Oh' Lord y'all got me preaching now!" Aunt Vye said as she rubbed the outside of her left leg right above her knee.

"There is no rush Auntie, take ya' time, I said take ya' time." Baby Boy laughed as he walked over to Maxine to show her an old track medal that he had in his hand.

"I just want y'all to know that a fine old lady like my-self needs about ten to fifteen minutes to get herself together. Little do y'all know, I may just run into my king down there at that hospital." Aunt Vye said as she pulled out a pocket mirror and lipstick before adjusting her blouse and wig to perfection.

"I know that's right." Maxine said.

"So you know a queen must stay fly, fly, fly, fly, fly, fly, fly." Aunt Vye said as she laughed, dipped back and kicked her leg out as she sat in the seat.

"Wait a minute. Wait a minute. Who is this fine young lady here? Joseph talk to me." Bryce asked as Denise walked into the room.

"Oh this my baby, my fiance. Denise this is my brother Bryce and this is my Aunt Vye." Baby Boy said as he abandoned talking to Maxine to run over to hug Denise.

"Oh this is my baby, my fiance. It's nice to meet you Denise." Bryce mimicked Baby Boy as he walked over to hug and greet Denise who stood about a foot shorter than him and his six foot four frame.

"Not to close, not to tight." Baby Boy said as he pulled Bryce's arm down and slid his hand in between the two.

"Fiance huh? Welcome to the family young lady." Aunt Vye said from across the room.

"Thank you Aunt Vye." Denise replied with a smile.

"Whoa'." Bryce, Baby Boy and Maxine all said.

"Maxine. I know she didn't just call me Aunt Vye? I know she just didn't call me Aunt Vye? Did she just call me Aunt Vye?"

"Yes she did." Maxine said as she tried to move over out of the way from Aunt Vye's path to Denise.

"Bryce did she?" Aunt Vye asked as she struggled to get up out of the love seat.

"She sure did." Bryce said as he moved Aunt Vye's bags of food to the other end of the table.

"I heard it too." Baby Boy said as he pulled his arm out of Denise's arms and pushed her out in front of him towards Aunt Vye.

"Oh I'm sorry. Miss Aunt Vye?" Denise said as she watched Aunt Vye finally stand up to walk towards her with her fist balled up.

"Girl I'm just joking. You can call me Aunt Vye sweetie." Aunt Vye said as she got closer and changed her facial expression to a smile and laughed as she walked up on Denise.

"Thank You." Denise said as she exhaled a sigh of relief.

"Now stop being so scared and give your new Auntie a hug." Aunt Vye said as she pulled her into her.

"Oh yes." Denise said.

"Welcome to the family baby. You got twenty dollars you can spot me?" Aunt Vye asked as she was hugging her.

"Aunt Vye, stop playing." Baby Boy yelled out as he ran over to pull Denise away.

"Boy I'm not playing. I came down here with a one way ticket, sixty eight dollars and these here expensive shoes. Girl you got twenty dollars?" Aunt Vye said as she pulled Denise back by her other arm.

"Sure, let me just go over here and get my bag." Denise said as she started to walk towards the couch where she left her duffel bag.

"Denise don't you give my Aunt no money." Baby Boy said as he watched Denise walk to the couch.

"Aunt Vye, leave that girl alone and let's go." Bryce said with a laugh as he cut short his private conversation with Maxine.

"I'll meet you guys there. I don't believe that Mr. Man here wants me riding in his jeep." Maxine said as she shook her head looking at Bryce.

"Don't start Max', because you know that you can ride right in the back seat of my truck any day." Bryce said as he winked at Maxine before stepping away with a devilish grin.

"Well okay." Baby Boy said as he watched Maxine and Bryce's exchange.

"Joseph I think I'm going to stay here with Maxine. You know I don't really do hospitals." Denise said as she looked up at Baby Boy from the couch.

"But baby I need you with me. I need you by my side." Baby Boy replied as he bent down on one knee in front of Denise.

"Aunt Vye, will you look at this?" Bryce said.

"I'm just saying." Baby Boy said as he placed her hand into his palm while rubbing it with his other.

"Baby I will be right here when you get back." Denise said as she ran her other hand over his head full of waves down the side of his face to stop at his strings of hair he called a beard.

"Okay if you insist." Baby Boy replied as he leaned his head to the side and pulled his body back in disappointment.

"I don't want to leave you snookums. I loves you. You knows I do." Bryce moaned to Aunt Vye as he slowly walked to her.

"And I don't want to leave you either snookie poo. Can I stay?" Aunt Vye said as she walked toward Bryce.

"You two are not funny. Snookie poo." Denise said as she sat up and pulled Baby Boy into her chest to hug him and kiss him on the top of his head.

"Later baby. Give me some sugar and don't you forget to miss me while I'm gone." Baby Boy said as he put his other knee down and puckered up his lips.

"Boy come get your butt in this car. You know she gon' miss you, I don't even know why you have to remind her." Aunt Vye said as she walked over and grabbed him by his collar to pull him up as Denise ducked back.

"Ain't that the truth." Bryce said.

"Oh I'm gon' give you some truth too. Wait til' we get outside." Aunt Vye said as she looked over at Bryce with her wig twisted to the side.

Here Comes The News

As we expected the entire ride to the hospital would be one big lecture from Aunt Vye and she didn't disappoint. She went from why Baby Boy would bring his girlfriend Denise to meet the family at such a time like this to how I talked to my wife. Baby Boy explained that no one could plan Dad getting sick and that he also had no money to buy his own plane ticket, and that Denise had offered to buy it for him if she could come. Aunt Vye took that as Denise being controlling and insecure. Baby Boy tried over and over to tell Aunt Vye that Denise was only being helpful and that she wanted to meet the family and to see New York. I was so detached from my brother that I had no clue that he was living off of soup, crackers and water while he was at school, and here I was trying to hold onto every penny because I never had much. My Aunt then decided to switch her attention over to me and my marriage and I kindly told her that my marriage was not up for discussion, and that everything will be alright. My Aunt then went on to call me everything but a child of God and made it clear that she was very disappointed in how all of my mother's children turned out. At this point I guess we weren't her brother's kids anymore. Now this was the same Aunt that had a different boyfriend or husband every two or three years, and the same Aunt that would choose a man over her kids. All of my cousins have totally disconnected themselves and their children from her. She never goes into that she hasn't seen her grandchildren in almost five years and they all live within hours of her. I know that she doesn't see how that she is in her own way of being loved and respected. The little that I do know about her and Dad's upbringing was that they were raised to guard their hearts and to not let anyone in under no circumstance for the fear of getting hurt. My mother always described my Aunt and Dad as hurt people, and she stressed that "Hurt people hurt other people".

"Dad does not look good. He does not look good at all." Sheryl said to Darlene as she paced back and forth in the waiting area room.

"Sheryl, don't get yourself all worked up. The doctor said that he would come out here and talk to us in about five minutes." Darlene said as she shook her asthma pump before spraying herself twice.

"Darlene, that was almost thirty minutes ago when he said that. You know what that means when these Doctor's stall right? Where is Bryce? Where is Joseph? They should be here. Darlene, I cannot take losing another parent. It hasn't been two years yet since we lost mommy." Sheryl said as she stopped in front of a sitting Darlene to pass her a bottle of water.

"Sheryl relax, Dad will be alright. We just have to pray through this okay? Try and stay calm. Bryce just went to pick up Aunt Vye, and they will be here soon." Darlene said as she untwisted the bottle cap to take a sip of water.

"Oh, I do not need to see her right now, as bad as she use to talk about Mama, and then had the audacity not to show up to her funeral! Hmm, talk about bad timing, today is not the day." Sheryl said as she sat down across from Darlene.

"Sheryl, that is all in the past. Buckle down and think about what about would God do? You have to be bigger than arguing with Aunt Vye."

"Darlene I am just not that good with sweeping things under the rug like you are." Sheryl said as she opened up a pack of gum and looking over at Darlene to offer her one.

"You mean forgiving people?" Darlene asked as she waived no to the stick of gum.

"No I meant exactly what I said, sweeping things under the rug."

My sister Darlene was known for either big heart or just being plain stupid to the truth. We could name situation after situation where she was wronged but chose to take the so called high road. Darlene has been through girlfriends sleeping with either her husband or boyfriend to co-signing for condos and cars for a boyfriend and her now ex-husband. To me there is no way that we can break up or get a divorce and you will be riding around better than me. I just can't see it. I don't know how you let someone keep a condo that you still have to help pay for because it has your name on it, credit attached to it and you living in a studio apartment.

"Sheryl you starting to sound just like Bryce." Darlene said.

"Hello ladies, I'm Dr. Johnson. Are you the King Family?" Dr. Johnson said as he entered the room walking straight towards Darlene.

"Hello Dr. Johnson, Yes. I'm Darlene King-Robinson and this is my sister Sheryl King." Darlene replied as she stood up while pointing at Sheryl.

"I am so sorry to have to meet you ladies like this."

"Is our father going to live?" Sheryl asked as she jumped up and stood next to Darlene.

"Yes he's going to live but.."

"What do you mean but?" Sheryl asked as she cut off Dr. Johnson before he could finish answering the last question.

"Sheryl, let the man talk. Doctor you were saying?'

"Your father needs a kidney transplant."

"No, no, no, no. Darlene I can't, I can't. I can't." Sheryl said as she stepped back away from the two of them.

"Sheryl, Dad is going to be okay. Isn't he doctor? Isn't he?"

"Mrs. King, without the surgery, your father won't live but for so long. He is retaining a lot of fluids, and he also has a urinary tract infection. Mrs. King his condition can get worse if we don't find..."

"I mean what can we do? What are our options?" Darlene asked as her face showed the worry.

"Well we can check the two of you to see if one of your kidneys is good enough to give to your father. Hopefully there's a match with one of you."

"Okay let's do it." Sheryl said as she stepped back closer.

"Dr. Johnson! We have two brothers, if we're no good or not a match. I'm praying to God that one of my brothers may be." Darlene said as she touched her stomach.

"Speak to them. Get your family together quick. You guys have some important decisions to make. I hope you guys are successful in your search. Get back to me as soon as possible. I will be either at the nurse's station or you can have one of the nurse's page me once you all have decided who and when you're ready to get tested. But let me remind you that time is running out. Let me get back to my patients." Dr. Johnson said as he started to walk off.

"Ladies, do y'all mind if I interject?" The Homeless Lady asked as she walked over.

"Miss I know you said you have a situation, but we are really, really going through something right now. So can you please leave us alone!" Sheryl yelled at her angrily.

"I'm sorry, I am so sorry. You are so right." The Homeless Lady said as she turned back around to walk to her seat.

"Miss what is your name?" Darlene asked the Homeless Lady as she took a few steps in her direction.

"Christine, Christine Maxwell from New Orleans. Born and raised."

"I'm so sorry Ms. Maxwell for my sister screaming at you, it's just that we.."

"It's no problem. All I was going to offer was that in times like this, maybe your family just needs to get together and pray. Pray just to see what it is exactly that God wants out of all this, because there are many ways to move forward, but there is only one way to stand still. And I know that in all things God works for the good of those who love him, and for those who have been called according to his purpose." The Homeless Lady said as she sat and tied one of her bags up before placing it under the bench seat.

"Yes you are right Ms. Maxwell, and I know that we will make it through this. I appreciate you for that." Darlene said as she stopped short from walking all the way over to the Homeless Lady.

"Young lady, the greatest gift that you can give some-one that is living, Is not to show them your riches, but to introduce them to theirs. Remember to pray, because you do know that prayer changes things. And you just watch, watch I say because God waits to the precise moment to come through with a miracle." The Homeless Lady said as she held up her bible up and looked up at the ceiling.

"Amen and yes he does, yes he does. Well I thank you Ms. Maxwell." Darlene said as she put her hands together as if she was praying and placed them over her mouth before waving bye.

"No need for the thanks. I just wanted to share that with you as God put it on my heart to do so." The Homeless Lady said as she nodded her head and put her bible in front of her heart.

"It's much appreciated trust me. Let me go over here to check on my sister and make sure that she is alright." Darlene said as she walked away.

Trying To Cope

I sat at the traffic light thinking of how Sheryl and I were the closest out of all of my siblings. I can say that Sheryl's love-hate relationship with Dad was our major bond. My sister always felt that Dad was embarrassed of her and her sexuality choice. He would never directly say to her that he hated her or her choice of lifestyle, but neither did he make her feel comfortable about it either. Sheryl would always cry about how she just wanted to be accepted in her own home at least. My mother did not agree with Sheryl's lifestyle but she never stopped loving her or being there for her when she did want to talk. Mama would tell me back then that a little girl's first relationship is with their father, and if that is missed out it could be very damaging to any young girl's idea of how she should be treated by a man. I didn't understand what my mother was sharing with me then and until this day I don't know if she felt that Dad's lack of interaction with Sheryl played a part in her becoming a lesbian. We had so many issues going on in one house that I was too scared to invite any of my friends over. It was definitely hard on me as the oldest child. There were times when Dad went out of his way to make me feel powerless by calling me names like "Soft", "A wimp" or a "Sissy" because at one point I had trouble sleeping at night and Mama would lay me in their bed until I finally fell asleep. I would get violently wakened up out of my sleep in the middle of the night sometimes as he came home from working the late shift. We would all hear the sounds of forced sex coming from out of their room as my mother would try to resist his often drunken requests. Darlene was called a "Cry Baby" by Dad because she cried over every little thing. I would have to agree with him on that because if you said boo in a room that was well lit she would cry, and if she fell and almost broke the skin on her knee, she would cry. Darlene cried if a band aid was on too tight. I believe that this is why she keeps everything in today. My sister now will not let you know that she is hurting on the inside and is comfortable with dealing with things in her own way. She is now a woman that won't obsess over her problems when she can be working on the solutions. I love that fact that she is more concerned with where she is going and not focused on where she came from. Sheryl got belittled all the time by Dad for believing that she was born like that. He would ask her, "How do you know what you like and don't like at such a young age?" There was never a time that he would let her answer, and I think that her not having an answer at the time or not answering was the best thing. And through all of this she still managed to somehow be a part time daddy's girl. We now joke on the phone when we talk about how she's changed and how the things that Dad said to her as a child helped her find comfort within her discomfort. Every conversation I would ask about her attitude changing and she would say there won't be any change coming to that and laugh. Sheryl tells me that she no longer involves herself with women but she still hangs out with her lesbian friends. I would tell her on the phone and to her face when we did meet for lunch that there is no way that she can still be around the same friends and not get tempted to go back and start doing her thing again. She felt like she had her time with women and had no regrets, and that she is taking her life into a different direction. She would also go on to say that she had no reason to stop being people's friend because she is no longer doing the things that they're continuing to do. I guess either she was telling me the truth or just giving me what she wanted me to know. I did exactly that to her whenever my marriage came up, because only me, Maxine and God knew that it was falling apart at the seams.

"Ooh that man kills me! Every chance he gets, he tries to embarrass me in front of his family." Maxine said to Denise as she walked into the living room and sat on the couch across from her.

"Maxine, what's wrong? What are you talking about?" Denise asked as she folded some of her clothes that she took out to put back into her suitcase.

"Bryce, I'm talking about Bryce. He gets on my nerves. Bryce is always calling his family and acting like everything is alright between us. Everything is far from alright. He lies to everyone, and now you too thinking that we this happy well to do couple." Maxine said as she sat on the couch with her arms folded.

"Tell me you joking." Denise asked as she stopped folding the clothes and tossed the rest into the suitcase.

"That's my husband and you know we haven't slept in the same bed in eleven months. Eleven months. That is a whole year Denise." Maxine said as she sat up and started redecorating the pictures and mats that were on the table.

"Eleven months is a long time." Denise said as she zipped closed her suitcase.

"Yes eleven months. And then on top of that he blames me for everything that is going wrong in his life. Everything!"

"But Joseph says he's so down to earth."

"Yeah he's down to earth alright, that man is so ver-bally abusive. It's the same as if he was hitting me." Maxine said as she picked up one of her and Bryce's wedding pictures.

"Wait Maxine, are you sure you should even be telling me this?" Denise asked as she unzipped the suitcase halfway to put in a shirt that she left out.

"Denise I've known this man since I was a teenager and I've been married to him for the last ten years. He has alienated me from my family." Maxine said as she sat back on the couch and started to rearrange the pillows.

"Maxine you are in charge of your own joy. I don't understand how do you cope? How can you survive if you freely giving up your happiness? Denise said as she walked over to sit down next to Maxine.

"I cope by encouraging myself. I survive through prayer. It's not easy Denise. Believe me it's tough. I guess I just have to keep on praying for him, praying for us."

"It sounds like you've lost yourself while trying to love him. Maxine you are no good to him if you are no good to yourself first. You doing all that praying, but are you praying for guidance?" Denise said as she grabbed Maxine's hand.

"Denise I pray for guidance, but sometimes I don't know if prayer is my steering wheel or if it's my spare tire." Maxine said as the tears started to form in her eyes.

"Prayer does help Maxine, but you have to be direct and consistent with your prayers. You know Joseph use to tell me that he would always find his mother praying. He said that she would cry out, that she claim her victory and that he knows that's how she got through by constantly talking to God. He said Mama would pray in her favorite pink and grey nightgown at the drop of a hat. He said Mama would get the sister's from her church and pray and that some nights they would all play sleep as Mama came in there room with her prayer rug and held church."

"Father, I call on you to be my strength. Father I need you to prick my husband's heart, Father according to

Psalms 51:10..: Please create in him a clean heart says Mama as she prepares the dinner table.

I need your strength Lord. Lord please work on this man. Father and help him to never raise his hand against me ever again. Father I call on you. Father I don't know how to be anymore faithful than I already am to you or this man. Please, please I'm asking you please, make me a candidate for a blessing. Father please make me a candidate for a blessing. Cover my family father, cover my family. Cover my children if anything. Amen." Mama prayed.

"He said he could always clearly hear his mother praying. Maxine it really is just a matter of you valuing your gift and your destiny, because not even an average farmer waits until their entire crop is gone or is unrecognizable to start pulling up the deadly weeds that are in it. So don't let nothing you do, anything your involved in or your marriage be destroyed before your eyes."

"Girl what are you studying in college, agriculture or mental health?" Maxine joked as she wiped away the tears.

"Neither, I am a political science major and I'm taking a few cyber space courses."

"Well I think you need to change your major."

"Maxine, Bryce has to respect you. I don't know one person that can truly love something or someone that they don't respect." Denise said as she put her hand on Maxine's shoulder while slightly shaking her.

"I know he loves me." Maxine said as she sat back with a pillow in her arms pressed against her chest.

"I believe that also, but does he respect you? Does he still cares about how he makes you feel? Does he still appreciate you?"

"Denise I can't even answer that."

"Well if you can't answer that then you need to think long and hard about where life is taking you instead of where life has you going."

"Denise I just pray that God deals with my needs, because it's my needs that make me desperate. I feel I need this man to live." Maxine said as she put her feet up on the couch to clutch tighter on the pillow.

"That's your husband and you are supposed to need him. But are you his wife?"

"He needs me." Maxine said as she stared at another one of her wedding photos that was sitting on the table inside of a broken frame.

"Please don't believe that just because you're needed that he won't leave you. That is when people leave us the most. Maxine you don't want to be just needed, you want to also be appreciated. Maxine people can hate who they need, people can despise who they need, but they can't hate or despise who they appreciate." Denise said as she touched Maxine's chin and turned her face towards her.

"Amen."

"Maxine If you want to pray right now, we can pray. Because when I first started dating Joseph, I asked God to handle my needs and once he did that he took the edge off of my desperation. Things have not been overall perfect but I am less desperate."

"Well girl, my needs have driven me to the point of desperation."

"That's right and for a while I had the power to wait." Denise said as she sat back and got herself comfortable in the corner of the couch.

"Yeah I bet that lasted for all about a week." Maxine said with a laugh.

"A week? Try about two or three days." Denise laughed as she reached behind her for a pillow.

"You are mess."

"I'm a work progress too, but God supplied my needs. Which was a greater understanding of who I was, and then he showed me what I really wanted out of the relationship. I fell, I picked myself. But I still.."

The telephone rings and Maxine answers "Hold on Denise. Hello. Yes I am in the King family. Oh no."

"Maxine what is it?" Denise asked as she put the pillow down next to her and moved closer to Maxine on the couch.

"It's Dad." Maxine whispered to Denise.

"How is he?"

"No, we'll be right there." Maxine said as she hung up the phone.

"How is he?"

"He's taken a turn for the worse and they can't contact Bryce. Can you call Joseph to find out where they are and how long will it be before they get to the hospital?" Maxine said as jumped up to run upstairs to get her car keys.

"Okay."

"I have to get to the hospital, so if you coming grab your stuff and let's go!" Maxine said as she ran down the stairs.

"I'm coming give me a second."

"Denise we don't have a second, you need to make that call and grab your coat at the same time." Maxine said as she threw on a thin light brown leather jacket from out of the hall closet and headed towards the front door.

"I'm right behind you." Denise said as she grabbed her school hoodie and ran behind Maxine.

Decision Time

After circling around in my truck for about fifteen minutes looking for a parking spot, I was finally walking into the hospital. I was still hesitant about being here and I was definitely not in the mood to hear any more of Sheryl's or Darlene's non-sense. As I walked down the hall my head managed to turn and look inside of every open door that I passed. I saw sick patient after sick patient, family member after family member huddled up in every room or there was a nurse standing behind a patient as they closed their night gown for them. It was a quiet walk too because I expected to hear my sister's mouths from all the way down the hall.

"Excuse me sir. How are you doing?" Bryce said to the doctor sitting behind the Nurse's station.

"Yes how may I help you?" Dr. Johnson asked.

"My name is Bryce King and I am looking for Joseph King's room." he asked as he leaned on the counter.

"Well we do have a Joseph King here, but may I ask what is your relationship to Mr. King?"

"My two sisters should be here with him."

"So he's your father?" Dr. Johnson asked as he reached to his left for a form.

"Look doctor I just need to catch up with my family. My sister's said that they were still here and I just dropped my brother and my aunt off to the main entrance." Bryce said as he tapped on the counter of the Nurse's station.

"Mr. King is in room 354 and he is not doing well. So if you plan on seeing him. You should do so within the next few hours." Dr. Johnson said as he looked all over the desk for a yellow highlighter.

"Nah doc'. I'm okay. I just want to see my family. I don't want to see that man. I'm not ready. Not right now!"

"Not right now? Mr. King I don't believe that your father is going to make it through the week, let alone past tomorrow." Dr. Johnson said as he stood up and placed two forms on top of the counter.

"He's doing that bad?"

"Yes he's doing that bad and he needs your support. Mr. King may just need to see your face or to even just hold your hand. You should go see him."

"I don't know doc'."

"Look I don't know the underlying situation between you two, but you should think about it. Don't give up on your father, because just when you are ready to give up, that's exactly when God is ready to show up."

"Let me do that. Let me just think. Because I really don't know if I want to see him honestly." Bryce said as he backed away from the Nurse's station.

"Bryce your father needs a kidney or he is going to die. And you just might be the only match for him."

"It's to that point?"

"It's to that point! You need to get tested to see if you are a match. I can test you right now." Dr. Johnson said as she pushed the forms on the counter towards the ledge.

"Why may I be the only match for him? Why me?"

"Well what are you going to do, when you don't know what to do? But you have to do something! If your Dad needs a kidney, and you can help, help him. At least get tested."

"You know something Dr. Johnson. I can't. I really can't.

I cannot find it in me to walk, to walk into that room and to see that man. Not yet, not just yet! Let me think." Bryce said as he stepped back to sit down on the bench and place his head against the wall.

"I don't understand." Dr. Johnson said as he walked from behind the Nurse's station to allow the janitor to clean.

"Son." Bryce hears his father's voice in his head from a conversation that they had years ago.

"Yes Dad?" Bryce replied.

"Bryce, I need you to be a better man than I have been.

Bryce please don't become the type of man that your father has been. Don't you ever, ever put your hands on a woman to harm her. Always love her, respect her, and treat her with class. Be better than your old man.

Son, Martin Luther King Jr. once said that "The ultimate measure of a man is not where he stands at in moments of comfort and convenience, but where he stands at in times of challenges and controversy." I need you to always stand up to the challenge."

"Yes Dad."

"Son I am sorry if I have shown you otherwise, because my faults as a father can become your faults as a man. Don't be like me son, strive to be better! And son?"

"Yes Dad?"

"If your grandfather was a janitor and I was raised to be the building's supervisor. I would want you to own the whole building and then continue to create that pathway for your children to own the entire block. Bryce it is alright for your dreams to be too big for your environment!"

"Yes I hear you."

"Bryce. Bryce. What are you going to do?" Dr. Johnson asked.

"Doc' I will be right back, let me just take a quick walk." Bryce said as he exhaled and stood up.

"Bryce we don't have the time to wait. His room is right this way."

"Give me a second Doctor." Bryce said as he started to walk away.

"You need to do decide something Bryce and you need to do it now." Dr. Johnson said as Bryce pushed open a stairwell door.

I never liked pressure and I hated more when someone mentioned that this man was my father. I knew I couldn't take his name off of my birth certificate, and I also didn't want nothing more than to hold a copy of his death certificate in my hands. How did I get such a cold heart towards him I was asked by a girlfriend when I was seventeen. I told her that I didn't know where to start, but I did tell her that his evil control over our house was killing everyone's spirit. And look now today, I may control whether he lives or not. And I think it's time he understands that yesterday's medicine can be today's poison.

"Excuse me, are you Dr. Johnson?" asked a lady walking from the other direction of the hallway.

"Yes that's me. How can I help you?"

"One of your nurses need you down here. They've been paging you!" The lady said.

"Thank you. Show me which room." Dr. Johnson replied as he headed down the hallway with the lady.

"You are the aunt." Darlene said to Aunt Vye as she followed her out of the waiting area room.

"Yes I am the aunt." Aunt Vye said to Darlene as she stopped walking and turned to face her.

"Then why are you going back and forth with Sheryl?"

"Ain't nobody going back and forth with that girl. That is a child only a mother could love." Aunt Vye said as she pointed her finger at Darlene's face.

"That's it. Sheryl is not a child anymore Aunt Vye."

"Well she sure does act like one. So what you should do is help me to get her to understand that I am the aunt. Because all I'm saying is there ain't nothing sweet over here. There ain't nothing sweet over here. I am from the projects and I can get projectish. Niece or no niece, she better ask somebody. Cause' I gets busy wit' these" Aunt Vye said as she rolled up her sleeves and put up her fist to show Darlene that she don't play.

"Hey I do believe we have a bigger situation here. Dad needs a kidney and y'all bickering about foolishness." Baby Boy said as he walked out into the hallway give Darlene her cell phone.

"The young man is correct. I need the names of those who are going to get tested. Mr. King needs a kidney and he needs one soon." Dr. Johnson said as he walked up to the three of them.

"Let me get down here to my brother's room. Because I cannot give you and this discussion of that Sheryl another second of my time." Aunt Vye said as she walked off.

"We're still waiting on one of you and your brother Bryce to decide on if they're going to get tested or not."

"Where is Bryce?" Darlene asked.

"He should be up here by now." Baby Boy said.

"He was here. He stopped at the Nurse's station and I asked him about possibly getting tested."

"So what's the hold up?" Darlene asked.

"Your brother Bryce is the hold up. He's not sure if he wants to get tested or not."

"He what?" Baby Boy asked.

"Paging Dr. Johnson. Paging Dr. Johnson. You're needed in room 354 Stat! You're needed in room 354 Stat!" we all heard blasted over the hospital intercom system.

"That's Dad's room." Everyone shouted before following Dr. Johnson as he took off running down the hallway.

The Truth

I felt like I had the worse life. I felt like my life was a string of bad decisions one after another or maybe I was cursed for being the child of this man. I went to the cafeteria for some peace and quiet and it was too crowded and noisy. I went to the main lobby to sit amongst everyone else, but there were no more seats. I decided to take the stairs and walk back up to the third floor and I finally found my quiet space to just sit and think. I was surrounded by several safety hazards which included a dripping water pipe and some well scattered cigarette butts but there was no one there to disrupt my peace. I was never a smoker or a drinker but at this moment I could sure use one of each. This little zone reminded me of my childhood when I would stare through the window guard and say to myself "If I could cross the street, I would run away". The best thing I could ever say about my childhood is that I survived it. All I could do at this moment was to ask myself. "What am I going to do?

Father help, for I am lost right now. Help me to understand why I feel this way about my own father?"

"That's because you are just like your father and it's tearing you up on the inside to go in that room and to see a piece of you. You cannot control your father's make-up or who he is, you just have to realize that sometimes "God will send you a great gift inside of some bad wrapping." Go and sit down with your father and try to work through his bad wrapping. I have been looking all over this building for you." Maxine said as she slowly walked up each step while holding onto the rail.

"Max please, you don't know what you're talking about." Bryce said as he stood up and opened the door to walk out into the hallway.

"Bryce, you can't keep running and you need to break yourself down before God does. Your day is coming!" Maxine said as says as she grabbed the un-held door from closing in her face.

"Where is everyone?" Bryce asked loudly as he entered the waiting area room.

"They're all probably in your father's room. Bryce, you can't run from or deny who you are, you just can't" Maxine said as she walked in behind him and stood right next to him.

"Bryce let's go, Daddy's not doing good and he is asking for you. We need you to come on." Sheryl said as she walked in and stood on the opposite side of Bryce.

"Okay, give me a minute Sheryl."

"Bryce let's go we don't have a minute. And oh yeah, Dad wants you to go and get Bryce Jr.!" Sheryl said as she walked out and turned back.

Bryce Jr., BJ as we called him. My son was more a conversation piece than he was a physical presence to our family. He was brought into this world by two young adults who had no business bringing a child into this world. Me and BJ's mother Karen were both in our twenties and neither one of us had a steady job, truly found ourselves or had any real intentions of raising a child. My Dad quickly spoke for my mother and said that they would play no part in raising BJ. This was my mistake and I should take care of it. Karen's mother decided without us to send her and the baby to Alabama by the time she reached her second trimester. When Karen and BJ did return to New York City, my child was born and now recognized as her cousin instead of her son. Not too long after their return, her mother decided to abandon New York and move everybody to North Carolina.

"Bryce Jr.? Did she just say? Tell me that I am hearing things!" Maxine asked as she grabbed Bryce and turned him around.

"What?" Bryce said as walked over and sat down.

"Now is not the time to play stupid or quiet. Did she just say that you have a son?" Maxine asked as she followed him to the seat and stood over him.

"Yes she said Bryce Jr., that's my son. My father's only living grandchild." Bryce said as he looked up at Maxine.

"Your son? Where did you get a son from Bryce?" Maxine leaned down and asked as she forcefully pulled Bryce's face up to look at her.

"Where do you think son's come from Maxine? Where do you think?" Bryce replied as he moved his face away from Maxine's hand.

"Don't you play with me, you know what I mean! This is not joke time. I need some answers! How old is this child? You have a son?" Maxine screamed as she grabbed Bryce by his sweater.

"The boy is.." Bryce tried to say while attempting to sit up.

"Your son? Bryce you have some explaining to do, and take that stupid look off your face." Maxine said as she pushed him back into the seat.

"Look I've been meaning to tell you." Bryce said as he jumped up to his feet.

"What you mean you've been meaning to tell me? You know how to tell me when you hungry and you use to know how to tell me when you wanted to be loved." Maxine said as she looked up at Bryce.

"Yes, and I've been meaning to tell. I just didn't know how to say it." Bryce said as he walked towards the door.

"Uhmm' excuse me like this, "Maxine I'm a no good man and I have a son named Bryce"" Maxine said in a deep voice as she stood up.

"Woman, don't you stand there and try to get ignorant on me." Bryce screamed out as he walked backed over to her.

"Fool, don't you walk up on me like you crazy. Not tonight black man, not tonight. Huh, just when I thought this marriage couldn't get any worse, you come with this." Maxine said as she pushed her fist into his chest.

"Maxine I never planned to hide this from you, but I guess I was just too scared to tell you." Bryce said as he tried to hug her.

"Don't touch me!" Maxine said as she smacked his hand away.

"Max'."

"Easy way out, huh! You know what, God needs to just remind you or rearrange your memory. He needs to take you back to your place of pain. Not so you could suffer, but so that you would never ever want go back there." Maxine said as she put her finger in his face.

"Max' I didn't want to let you down, nor did I want you to find out this way!"

"How could I have not found out, everything comes out eventually Bryce. Bryce I have never kept a secret from you. I've never. I have never ever even lied to you. Bryce you have broken my heart time and time again into little, little pieces. And my dumb butt, I still even tried to love you with all the little broken pieces." Maxine said as she sat down and put her face into her hands.

"Max' I need you right now, please don't do this. Not here, not right now. Let's not get crazy" Bryce said as he kneeled down on one knee in front of her.

"It's always about you, and I'm far from crazy. But I am the fool for putting up with your nonsense for all these years." Maxine said as she began to cry and pushing Bryce from in her front of her as she got up.

"Come here." Bryce said as he reached for her.

"Bryce don't touch me."

"You see how you do! I said come here." Bryce said as he got up off of his knees to walk after her.

"Bryce if you put your hands on me. You are going to be in one of these hospital rooms too! I'm not playing with you because I will cut you deep, wide, and consecutively. And I promise you that." Maxine said as she turned to point at Bryce as he walked up on her.

"Look I'd still be an honest man to you, if Sheryl wouldn't have opened her big mouth!" Bryce said as he stopped from walking towards her.

"Honest man, you think you'd still be an honest man? Boy I told you from the first day that you met me, just tell me the truth. Tell me the truth. Bryce if you just only tell the truth, you don't have to remember a thing!

But once you start lying!" Maxine said as she walked towards Bryce as he sat down.

"You don't understand the situation." Bryce said as he sat back and looked around the room.

"No you don't understand the situation!" Maxine leaned over to him and whispered.

"And what is the situation Max'?" Bryce yelled as he stared up at her.

"The situation is I tried to put a temporary person into a permanent position." Maxine growled as she put each hand on an arm rest and leaned forward closer to him.

"So I'm temporary now?" Bryce asked as he inched up to come face to face with her.

"I made you a priority Bryce, and what did you do? You made me an option! I was so caught up in getting married, that I never thought about just waiting on the one that God had for me." Maxine said as she pulled back and took a few steps back.

"Whatever Max', I'm going to go and get my son. We'll handle this later." Bryce said as he got up and walked up to her face.

"Don't you walk away from me Bryce King. This is just the beginning and there may not be any later." she screamed as she walked behind him to turn him around.

"You just told me not to put my hands on you."

"I need some answers, and I am going to get them now."

"Max', it was a long time ago and I'm sorry. I've done wrong, but how can I right it now Max'? How can I make this right?" Bryce flailed his arms and asked.

"I don't care if it was last week Bryce. You hid this child from me, your child. If you would've been straight up with me from the beginning, you would've known how I would've supported you or not!" she said as she walked up to Bryce.

"Look, I'm not dealing with his mother anymore, that chapter of my life is over with." he said as he walked right pass her to go sit back down.

"And I'm just supposed to believe you after finding out that you can keep your own flesh and blood a secret? You practically denied your own." she said to Bryce as she followed him to the seat.

"Yes, I need you to believe me. Maxine, this all was before you."

"Oh yeah the baby was before me, but the lies were to me. I want to meet her!" she said as she stood over him waiting for an answer.

"Excuse me, meet her who?" Bryce asked as he looked up.

"The child's mother, I want to meet her!"

"I have not spoken to that woman in over three years. She doesn't want anything to do with me. She claimed that I treated her daughter differently than I treated Bryce Jr."

"Oh this is way too much. So now you have two kids?" Maxine asked as she put her hands on her hips before walking away.

"No. I said her daughter. She has a child from another relationship and berated me all the time for loving my own child more than hers, she said I was played favorites. That's why we broke up the last time we dated!" Bryce said as he stood up to walk over to Max'.

"I don't believe you, get out of my sight." Maxine said before pushing him away.

"Max'."

"Bryce. Bryce." Maxine screamed to him as he walked out.

"Let him go." The Homeless Lady said.

"I can't believe these people! As good as I've been to this family, as good as I've been to this man, and no one told me he had a son." Maxine said out loud to herself as she paced through the waiting area room.

"Where's my brother?" Sheryl asked as she entered the waiting area room.

"He left." Maxine said as she sat down.

"What you mean he left? He left to go where? Did you chase him off? My father is in there sick and.."

"Girl, don't you come out here and try to jump down my throat!" Maxine yelled as she jumped up to her feet.

"Maxine please."

"I just had my heart ripped out of my chest with this Bryce Jr. mess."

"Why, because Bryce has a son? Something that you can't give him." Sheryl said as she walked up to Maxine.

"Sheryl you don't know what I can or can't give my husband. But you could've said something to me about this child." Maxine said as she stared at Sheryl face to face.

"Maxine I do not like you and trust me I have been dying to tell you." Sheryl replied as she brought her nose up close to Maxine's nose.

"Where's Bryce?" Darlene asked as she entered the waiting room area as Sheryl and Maxine stood face to face.

"He left! Miss Hollywood -soap opera- actress here ran him off!" Sheryl said as she backed up and turned to Darlene.

"He what?" Darlene said.

"Yeah he left. He went to go get his son little Bryce Jr. So now the whole family can all be here. I guess the family that lies together, should cry together." Maxine said as she looked at Sheryl up and down.

"We should do what?" Sheryl said as she stepped towards Maxine.

"Sheryl stop it. So you know now?" Darlene said as she grabbed Sheryl's arm.

"Now I do. No thanks to you Darlene."

"Yes she knows now, because I told her!" Sheryl said from behind Darlene.

"Sheryl that was not your place!" Darlene yelled as she turned to Sheryl.

"I know it wasn't." Sheryl said as she turned to walk to the door.

"And I told you before you left that room to not mention that child." Darlene said to Sheryl as she waved her off.

"Well, why didn't you tell me Darlene? We have been best friends for too long and you knew for years that I could not have kids because of what my mother's boyfriend use to do to me" Maxine said as she approached Darlene.

"Yes I know Maxine. We've been friends for over thirty something years, since the first grade."

"That's right, thirty something years. And I was the one who was there for you when we were sixteen. Sixteen years old Darlene remember?" Maxine said as she looked into Darlene's face.

"Maxine not now, don't do this." Darlene said as she sat down with her hand placed on her head.

"Sixteen Darlene, do you remember when you would always come to me telling me that your father was touching on you. I kept those secrets to protect you, to protect your family." Maxine said as she sat down next to Darlene to talk into her face.

"Maxine." Darlene said.

"I guess you were protecting me too huh?" Maxine asked.

I wish I was there to have protected my wife when she was raped over and over by her mother's boyfriend back then. The effects of her being violated by that man haunt her to this day. She has her nights where she wakes up screaming. She has her moments where she feels she ruined her mother's life by exposing what was going on to her. But she hurts most by the damaged her uterus suffered and how easily she the trauma comes back when we make love. And she always believed that Darlene possibly made up the story about Dad abusing her to make her feel like she wasn't alone.

"Shut your mouth Maxine! Don't you talk about my father like that! Darlene what is she saying?" Sheryl said from the doorway.

"No I'm not shutting up!" Maxine said as she continued to face Darlene.

"My father would not." Sheryl said as she slowly walked over to Darlene and Maxine.

"Yes Sheryl, What she's saying is true!" Darlene said as she lifted her head up to look at Sheryl.

"No, no, no. It can't be. You two are making this up. Y'all just want to kick daddy while he's down. Not my father, not my father, he would never, he would never." Sheryl screamed as she stopped and turned to walk out.

"Sheryl wait! Sheryl." Darlene screamed as she jumped up to chase behind Sheryl.

Family Stays Together?

I decided to leave all of the chaos of the hospital behind for about an hour or two. I just needed to get in my truck and ride. I was headed to the other side of town to go and get my son. I figured that I could at least let him see his grandson walk into that room as he requested, and hey I may just even go in there myself. I wasn't to hell bent on letting the doctor's cut on me. It's not that I don't want to save his life, I just don't think that he is worth me risking mines. The calls and the texts having been coming from my sisters non-stop since I left and the last voicemail that Darlene left said that the doctors had insisted that the family go home and relax since they somehow got Dad stabilized. She said that Dr. Johnson promised that he would be there and would be monitoring Dad himself. She also said that he was waiting for a few calls on some possible donors and looking to hear from me. I haven't heard my sister cry in years. But she cried on my voicemail as if her world was just turned upside down. She didn't even cry at Mama's funeral, but she did have her time to grieve afterwards. With the way that she was talking on my voicemail I knew that the doctor possibly shared more with her than she was telling. A small part of me wanted to drive over to Memorial Hospital and check up on Leah, but I knew that I had to get my mind right and bring closure to this situation with my family before I even thought about addressing anything else. It was time for me to call my family and tell them that I couldn't do it. I won't even get tested.

"What is going on here? What did I come home to? Darlene? Aunt Vye? We use to be a close and loving family. Somebody tell me something" Baby Boy asked as he circled the room looking at everyone one by one.

"Baby Boy relax, let's get your father, my brother straight and we can take care of all this madness later." Aunt Vye replied as she sat back eating on a piece of cake.

"Well, I cannot give daddy my kidney because of my past drinking habits.

I knew I should've taken myself to rehab." Darlene said as she sat next to Aunt Vye.

"Is that what the doctor's told you?" Denise asked.

"They tried ta' get you to go to rehab, but you said no, no, no." Aunt Vye singed to Darlene.

"Pretty much yes, that's what the doctor said. I guess all that drinking to compensate for my pain has finally caught up to me." Darlene said as she looked at Aunt Vye as if she was crazy.

"Girl and I am so glad for you that God has cleaned you out, because you use to drink like a fish." Aunt Vye said as she laughed and made a gargle sound.

"Funny." Darlene said.

"Pay me no mind baby."

"Trust me I'm trying not to." Darlene said as she slid over on the couch away from Aunt Vye.

"Did anyone hear back from Bryce?" Denise asked.

"The last we heard, he was headed to get his son." Aunt Vye said as she took the last bite of her cake out of the napkin.

"He just texted me back and he said that he was on his way back to the hospital from trying to get BJ." Darlene said.

"Maybe we should all go back to the hospital." Baby Boy said.

"The doctor said that we should relax here at home since they got Dad's urinary tract infection under control." Darlene said to Baby Boy as she took off her shoes to relax her feet.

"Darlene I hear you but I just don't feel comfortable sitting here while your father is there alone." Aunt Vye said as she wiped the crumbs off of her shirt in into her hand.

"Aunt Vye there isn't much we can do at the hospital." Darlene replied.

"Besides argue." Baby Boy replied.

"Well I'm from the old school and I know your father felt our presence while we were there." Aunt Vye said.

"I don't know why Sheryl mentioned anything about that child in front of Maxine?" Darlene said as she pushed her shoes over to the side with her feet.

"She did what?" Baby Boy asked.

"You know that girl can't even hold cold water. I don't know why y'all even mentioned him being picked up." Aunt Vye said as she started to tie her head scarf around her wig.

"Wait, so he really did leave to go and get BJ? So I do have a nephew? Baby Boy asked.

"Yeah, that's his child. Boy got his head and his attitude." Darlene replied.

"How old is that boy anyway?" Aunt Vye asked as Sheryl walked in.

"He should be around ten or eleven now right Darlene?" Baby Boy asked.

"How come you didn't tell me about Dad, Darlene? How could you keep that from me? I don't believe you! I don't believe this nonsense one bit." Sheryl said as she stood in front of Darlene.

"Because, I didn't want you to look at Dad no different that was my fight." Darlene said to Sheryl as she looked up at her.

"Look at him no different? He's a monster if what you're saying is true."

"What are y'all talking about?" Baby Boy asked.

"Your father, we talking about your father." Sheryl said as she turned to look at Baby Boy.

"This looks juicy." Aunt Vye said as she sat up on the other end of the couch.

"Denise can you excuse us for a minute?" Sheryl asked as she looked across the room to her.

"No she's family now. Whatever you have to say, she can hear it!" Baby Boy said as he put his hand on her shoulder as he sat on the arm of the couch next to her.

"Joseph!" Darlene said.

"I said no, she's family now."

"Look baby, I don't want to cause anymore tension or bring more friction to a scene that has enough of both. I can go upstairs for a few." Denise said as she looked up at Baby Boy.

"Sweetie sit tight."

"Let her go upstairs Baby Boy." Sheryl said.

"No she can stay right here. You tell everything else Sheryl and don't care who you hurt. What is going on? I'm tired of being in the dark in this family about every-thing."

"Okay. Well Dad use to touch on Darlene." Sheryl said as she backed away from Darlene.

"What?" Everybody said at the same time.

"Allegedly!" Sheryl said as she backed completely away from Darlene.

"Not my brother, Sheryl you got it twisted. Sheryl where you get this foolishness from? Darlene what is she saying?" Aunt Vye asked.

"Ask your favorite niece Darlene." Sheryl replied.

"Darlene what is she saying?" Aunt Vye asked as she moved over to sit next to Darlene.

"She got it from me and it's true! Do I dislike dad for what he's done? Yes. Do I hate him and wish for a devils hell? No." Darlene said as she began to cry.

"Wait a minute now. Let's just wait one minute here. Let me make sure that I am hearing this right. You telling me that Joseph King Sr., my brother, your father touched you?" Aunt Vye asked Darlene as she moved her hands from over her face.

"Allegedly!" Sheryl blurted out.

"Yes." Darlene said.

"Now you know this is crazy right Darlene. You see y'all done got my pressure up right now, somebody go in that fridge and get me a pickle." Aunt Vye said as she sat back in disbelief.

"Mama tried to kill Dad the night that I told her. She kicked him out and told him to never come back." Darlene said as she cried and rocked back and forth.

"Darlene, Darlene, Why now. Why are we hearing about this now?" Aunt Vye asked.

"Me and Mama stayed up all night crying and praying as she washed and held me in the bathroom."

"Darlene, I will protect you! God will protect you. If he even thinks of touching you again, I'll kill him. Be strong Darlene. Be strong for those who cannot be strong for themselves. Do you understand me?" Mama said.

"Yes Mama, I understand you."

"Good. Now you be sure to pray for me and this family. Lord knows that I could use the prayers. It's taking a toll on me as a saved woman to try and keep this family together. I need the strength. Help us Lord, because we still have the faith in you. But tonight Lord, can you please help me show Satan that this household that you lead is better to you than any of his followers are to him. Protect us Lord. Protect us."

"Mama saw to it that we were safe, she prayed for us all." Darlene said.

"Mama did whatever she had to do to make sure that we ate and that we went to school and church." Baby Boy said as he looked at both of his sisters.

"Yes she did, and she always reminded us that we could do all things through Christ who strengthens us. I sure do miss Mama." Darlene said as she stood up to walk out with her face in her hands and her head down.

"We need to pray for your father and we need to pray for Darlene." Denise said.

"You see that's why I love you. You always know what to say." Baby Boy said.

"You right young lady, you're absolutely right. We have to keep them both up in prayer, because this is all too much madness." Aunt Vye said as she looked over at Sheryl.

"You know what I'm going to do it. I'm going to give Dad my kidney." Baby Boy said as he looked at Denise.

"God's going to bless you for that son, but think about your future now before you rush to judgment." Aunt Vye said.

"That's big of you Baby boy. You know by doing what you're doing, you are potentially giving up your dreams of making it to the NBA. You do know that right?" Sheryl asked.

"That's right we need to think." Denise said as Sheryl and Aunt Vye looked at her.

"Yes, I know, but I need my father more than anything.

What's making it to the NBA if your Dad can't even see you play in it?"

"We need to pray, and we need to pray right now." Denise said as she looked at Sheryl and Aunt Vye.

"Yeah we need to pray alright. Talking about "That's right we need to think"." Sheryl said as she stared at Denise until she turned her eyes away.

"I didn't mean it like that." Denise said to Aunt Vye.

"I know you didn't mean it like that baby." Baby Boy said.

"I just can't receive that my brother, would touch on one of his own kids like that." Aunt Vye said as she reach out at Baby Boy to signal to him to help her get up.

"Allegedly!" Sheryl said.

"Let's all join hands while I'm up." Aunt Vye said as she looked at Denise.

"Sheryl you come over here and stand between me and Denise please." Baby Boy said.

"Good call Boy." Aunt Vye said as she gave Baby Boy a head nod.

"Boy plays on Tarzan." Baby Boy said to Aunt Vye.

"Well swing over and grab cheetah hand." Aunt Vye said as she pulled her hand back as if she was going to pop him.

"Can we pray now?" Denise asked.

"Let's bow our heads. Father I call on you now to be our strength." Aunt Vye said as she began the prayer.

Look Inside Yourself

It was a little after eight o' clock and I had just fin-
ished the prolonged conversation about the visiting hours
being almost over with the lady at the help desk in the
lobby before getting a pass to come up. I just left from
another debate with BJ's mother Karen as I picked him
up. She decided that now was the time to discuss if I
could send her more money than what I have been
sending and when will I start to spend more time with my
child. She was totally neglecting the fact that his grandfather wanted to see him before his condition got worse.
She was right in saying that no one in my family has
taking the time to reach out to ask how he is doing, if he
needed anything or shown a desire to see him in the ten
years that he has been on this earth. She was totally right
and I just yessed her to death so that I could get my son
and leave. I respected everything that she said because her
main and only care was that our son had a father in his
life and that I took care of my responsibilities financially.
While we were at the help desk she called to make sure

that I didn't let BJ see my father if it was too late and to remind me that he also had school in the morning. Once we finally got to Dad's room we were greeted by a team of doctors who said that we could not enter into his room. They gave me no explanation or showed no interest in telling me what was going on inside the room or with him. All they would repeatedly say was that I had to go to the nurse's station and speak to either Dr. Johnson or to any nurse working on this floor. As me and BJ walked up to the Nurse's station we could see Dr. Johnson with his face in his hands leaning down behind the counter.

"God take my hand. God take control. Guide me through this day when I don't have the strength or the wisdom to do it myself." Dr. Johnson whispered to himself as he sat in the chair at the Nurse's station.

"Dr. Johnson. Dr. Johnson. Is everything okay? I want to uhmm'. I want to have a few words with my father, but the doctors standing outside of his room door said to come see you first. Is there something wrong? I thought he was stabilized?" Bryce asked as he leaned on the counter of the Nurse's station.

"Yes there is something wrong. Your father has been slipping in and out of consciousness."

"No, No he can't! I need to speak to him. I'm ready. I need closure.

His grandson is here, I need us three to connect."

"Dad, what's wrong with Granddad? Where is he?" BJ asked as he pulled on his father's shirt.

"Granddad is still sick son, he's sleeping right now." Bryce said as he looked over at BJ.

"But I wanna' see him, Dad I wanna' see him. He owes me five dollars."

"Ok, you will. You will see him son and I'll make sure he gives you your five dollars."

"Bryce. It may be too late. We tried, we asked, we searched, but in the waiting is where we failed. I'm sorry. I have to go now." Dr. Johnson said before walking off.

"Dad, what was all that mumbo jumbo the man was saying?" BJ asked with a puzzled look on his face.

"Son, what the Doctor pretty much was saying is that.."

"What he's saying young man, is that there are sometimes unanswered questions and man-made mountains that should only be valleys. And you must be Little Bryce."

"Now I'm really confused!" BJ said as he looked at both Bryce and Maxine.

"BJ, this is my wife Maxine." Bryce said as he put his hand on Maxine's shoulder.

"Wife like as in girlfriend? Wow Dad. She's pretty."

"No wife like as in wife. And thank you young man, you're pretty handsome yourself!" Maxine said as he put her hand on top of BJ's head.

"She's aight." Bryce said with a laugh.

"Excuse me?" Maxine said as she half smiled at Bryce.

"Nah son, she's one hundred percent beautiful inside and out."

"Don't you try to get on my good side now, because you are not in the clear yet. Listen, you go check on your Dad. I tried to and they wouldn't let me into his room. They said that there only allowing his children into his room."

"I tried, but they wouldn't let me either."

"Maybe it's because you had you BJ with you. Leave him here with me and try again."

"Okay, okay, just keep an eye on my boy for me."

"He will be okay. You just go and check on your father." Maxine said as she tried to brush Bryce off with a hand gesture.

"BJ you holler if you need me. I don't care if you have to scream through this hospital for help." Bryce said as he squatted down to grab BJ by the shoulders.

"Go ahead Bryce! He will be alright." Maxine said as she tapped on Bryce's arm.

"Alright, alright. BJ, if you need me." Bryce said as he looked up at Maxine and then back at BJ.

"Dad I'm a big boy. I'll be alright." BJ said as he puts a hand on each of his father's arms.

"Okay. I will see both of you in a minute." Bryce said as he stood up, rubbed the top of BJ's head and turned to walk down the hall.

"Listen, BJ, Would you mind if I call you LB? Little Bryce. I don't like BJ. I think LB is a little cooler." Maxine asked as she pulled BJ into her side by his shoulder as they watched Bryce walk down the hall.

"Yeah that's cool with me. What can I call you?" BJ asked as he looked up at Maxine as she looked downward at him.

"Aww, you can call me Maxie." she said as they walk into the waiting area room.

"Maxie. Okay Maxie."

"Now LB, I want you to listen to me and I want you to listen to me good." Maxine said as they both sit down in the first seats that they came across.

"Yes Mamm', I mean Maxie."

"Ooh, I like you. You are so well mannered. LB, in your lifetime you only get one mother. I want you to promise me, promise me that you will always listen to your mother, regardless of her faults, bad decisions and all of her mistakes."

"I will. I promise. Look my fingers aren't even crossed. I'm telling the truth! I promise I'll listen."

"And always LB, always respect women. Learn to be nice to them. Sometimes you may have to be better to them than they are to themselves."

"You mean love them? Like my father loves you!"

"Boy, Love ain't nothing but a misunderstanding between two fools." Maxine said with laugh.

"Maxine, call the house and tell everyone to get over here now. The doctors are going to perform emergency surgery on me in a hour to try and save Dad. The testing came back and I'm a perfect match." Bryce said as he ran into the room clearly out of breath.

"Dad I wanna' go with you, I love you." BJ said as he jumped up to hug his father.

"BJ I Love you too. But I need you to stay here with Maxine while I go help Granddad. Maxine, I love you. Pray for me." Bryce said as his eyes begin to water.

It was time. It was time for me to finally do the right thing. I realized that if I could make a difference and try to move forward; now was the time. I listened to Maxine forgive her mother's boyfriend. I listened to Darlene forgive all those that have wronged her and I witnessed Mama do more than her fair share of forgiving. So why couldn't I do it. Besides, the forgiveness is for me and not for Dad. I can save my Dad's life. I have my wife here by my side and a opportunity to reconnect with my son. All of this from one hospital visit. This is nobody but God.

"Bryce! I love you too baby. I'm here for you." Maxine said as she got up to hug Bryce as well.

"I love you both. Now stay here with Max' BJ. I have to go help Granddad." Bryce said as he kneeled down to kiss BJ on his forehead.

"You are always leaving me Dad." BJ said as he hugged and watched a tear fall out of his father eye.

"I'm not leaving son, I'm just going to help stop Granddad from being sick." Bryce said as he patted him on his back.

"Come on LB. Dad will be right back. Go Bryce." Maxine said as she placed her hands on BJ's shoulders after wiping away the tears that trickled down her cheeks.

"Thanks Max'. I'll be right back son." Bryce said as he stood up and walked out of the waiting area room.

"Hey, Dad" BJ called out as he ran to the door to after his father.

"Yes son." Bryce replied as he turned around to answer BJ.

"Good luck and don't forget my five dollars." BJ said as he winked at his father.

When Times Are Difficult

I had made the choice. The choice to do what was right. I had no clue as to how things were going to turn out, but I knew I was doing the right thing. "Where was my family at?" I wondered. For the first time in my life I was actually doing the right thing and now no one was around for me to show them. As I changed into the hospital clothing that I had to wear for the surgery I was hoping that Maxine was able to get through to everyone so that they could be here praying for us before the surgeries begun.

"Did anybody see that fried turkey Maxine started cooked sitting on the top of that stove?" Baby Boy asked as he entered the living room from the kitchen entrance.

"Yes, Yes and you know ya' Aunt Vye is ready to get at it." Aunt Vye said as she sat her can soda on the end table while rubbing her hands together.

"Yeah, we know you are!" Sheryl said as she rolled her eyes.

"You know ya' Mama would never beat you for that mouth of yours. But I'll give you what you need. I'm telling you, I will give you exactly what you need."

"Come on now. We are all saved women here." Darlene said as she looked at both Sheryl and Aunt Vye.

"Well her savings are running low and she needs to restock up on her J.C."Aunt Vye said.

"J.C.?" Darlene asked.

"Yes J.C.. Oh not the drink. I'm sorry Darlene. I meant Jesus Christ.

"You not right Aunt Vye." Denise said as she laughed.

"Excuse me." Aunt Vye said.

"I meant Ms. Aunt Vye."

"That's better, because you know there ain't no party like a holy ghost party, cause a holy ghost party don't stop."

"No we ain't gon' have none of that. We just gon' pray for her to get some Christian coupons and for her to get her savings back right." Darlene said as she walked away from Aunt Vye.

"Ladies, can't we all just get along? Look I'm going to get some deserts to rock with Maxine's turkey. Can we have a nice family dinner tonight before we head back over to the hospital? Is that too much to ask for?" Baby Boy asked as he looked at everyone and tried to force a smile out of them all.

"No it is not too much to ask for Baby Boy. And yes we will have a nice family dinner together. Won't we ladies? Darlene asked as she received complete silence from all of the ladies.

"Now everybody don't speak at the same time. Can we please let this house be in one piece when I return?" Baby Boy said to a room with complete silence.

"Bye boy, and pick me up a bag of skins and a diet coke on your way back." Aunt Vye said as she shifted in her seat to reach for her bag of candy that was sitting on the table.

"And what's the diet coke for?" Sheryl asked.

"Make that two diet cokes. I want you to add one for my favorite nephew Sheryl sitting right there." Aunt Vye said with sarcasm while looking at Sheryl.

"I got ya' nephew." Sheryl said as she grilled Aunt Vye.

"I'm out. I can't with y'all." Baby Boy said.

"Could you two stop for at least five minutes?" Darlene asked.

"It's not me." Aunt Vye said.

"It's never neither one of you." Darlene replied as she looked at Aunt Vye and then at Sheryl.

"What?" Sheryl said as Darlene looked at her.

"Whew. Finally a moment with us girls alone. I need to talk to y'all. I need some advice, some help." Denise said as she looked out the window to make sure that Baby Boy was gone.

"Girl, what is it now?" Sheryl asked.

"I've been struggling in this area of my relationship with Joseph. All this man wants to do is have sex, sex, sex, and I just cannot do it anymore.

I've made a decision to stay holy and as a saved woman I want to stay correct. I need Joseph to be my soul mate, because I am no longer interested in having a flesh mate." Denise said as she walked back to the couch to sit down.

"Do you think we want to hear about our little brother's sex life. I know I don't." Darlene asked as she took a bite out of her sandwich.

"Baby I had to get delivered from fornicating a few times." Aunt Vye said as she sat back and crossed her legs.

"Now that's nasty." Sheryl said as she turned her body away from Aunt Vye's direction.

"Oh yes it is." Aunt Vye said in a slow and sexy tone while looking at Sheryl.

"Ladies I'm serious" Denise said as she moved up to the edge of the couch and looked at everyone.

"Okay seriously baby. What you have to do is pray." Aunt Vye said.

"Pray." Darlene sung as she walked over to Sheryl.

"We pray." Aunt Vye singed.

"Pray." Darlene singed as she nudged Sheryl.

"We pray." Aunt Vye singed as she sat up and wiggled.

"Pray." Darlene singed to Sheryl as she pushed her away.

"We have to pray just to make it today." Aunt Vye and Darlene sung together.

"You crazy Aunt Vye. I mean Ms. Aunt Vye. But seriously, singing Mc Hammer is not going to work in the heat of the moment." Denise said as she looked at Aunt Vye and Darlene perform and laugh.

"Well it's better to be hot and bothered on any night than to be sitting around cold and worried on a following morning. You just be careful, because some mistakes can't be reversed." Aunt Vye said as she plopped down onto the couch.

"And you describing your sex life is a mistake and it is bothering me." Sheryl said as Aunt Vye looked at her with her fist pointed towards her.

"It's okay Denise, just try and keep Jesus on your mind. Stay with the Lord Denise, he is the only way." Darlene said as she sat down next to Denise while trying to catch her breath.

"Look I'm not asking something as crazy as do Christian's make love to gospel music? I'm struggling here." Denise said to the ladies as she look at them all.

"I use to." Aunt Vye said.

"What struggle?" Denise asked.

"No. Make love to gospel music."

"Aunt Vye." Darlene yelled out as she hit her leg and stared at her.

"What. Don't judge me." Aunt Vye replied as she pulled on the two hairs that she had on her chin.

"We gon' pray for you Aunt Vye." Darlene said as she could not think of any words to say to her Aunt.

"Pray, pray, pray. Aunt Vye, Darlene I am so prayed up it's a shame. Joseph has to marry me. No ring. No queen. Never!" Denise said as she look next to her to tell Darlene.

"Girl, what you mean you never? No more sex?" Sheryl asked.

"That's right Sheryl never! No more sex for me and Joseph."

"Denise if it means your soul. I totally understand." Darlene said.

"But with all these fast girls chasing behind him at our university I feel like my back is against a wall, just to try and keep him focused on me. I don't know how to fight them."

"That's all they are Denise, is girls. In all seriousness, you girl, you stay Holy! If my nephew can't holdout, you do what you gotta' do and you stay holy." Aunt Vye said.

"Denise, what you have to realize is that you can say no to a good thing, if it is not consistent with where you are trying to go. It's called the art of waiting. How can I not do the right thing at the wrong time?" Darlene said.

"It's hard. I don't understand because I'm so disciplined in other areas. But this sex thing has me off balance." Denise replied.

"You right Denise it is hard, because I feel like I'm living between a rock and a hard place sometimes. I mean we are still human and the devil is working overtime on my flesh." Sheryl said as she looked at Aunt Vye.

"Uh huh. Overtime is right, but he working seven and a half days a week on me. What. Why y'all looking at me? Like your Aunt Vye ain't sexy?

Oh, y'all don't think that your Aunt Vye still got it? Don't sleep, because I can still drop it like it's hot."

"Or let it down like its warm!" Sheryl said as she laughed and looked over at Aunt Vye.

"I know that's right auntie. You may just need to show her how to drop it." Darlene said while laughing.

"No she does not." Sheryl said.

"Please don't anyone drop a thing. What I need you all to do is to help me, because I am confused." Denise said.

"You not confused. You just looking for some reassurance that you are about to do the right thing." Darlene said as she sat back on the couch to eat the rest of her sandwich and sip on some tea.

"I am confused because I go to these forums at my church and they field our questions but.."

"But what?" Sheryl asked as se cut off Denise.

"I was trying to tell you."

"I know over at my church we had a ladies retreat once, and I asked, what do I do when it's late at night and my body and my mind start talking to me? You know what I'm saying, it's like my mind and body be playing tricks on me." Darlene said as she sat her tea and sandwich down on the table in front of her to move her body and show everyone how she felt.

"Uh huh, uh huh." Aunt Vye said as she sat up and cheered Darlene on.

"You know all I was told was to just read some scriptures. I looked at that lady and said Sister, reading some scriptures is just not going to cut it every time. I need deliverance!" Darlene said as she sat down with a disappointed look on her face.

"Who are you telling?" Sheryl said.

"It sure does take more than just some scriptures sometimes." Denise said.

"Shoot most of the time." Aunt Vye said.

"Right and I don't want stay programmed. A scripture for this, and a service for that!" Denise said as she looked around at everyone's facial expression.

"Church on this day. Church on that day." Sheryl added.

"We have to give God more, because I'm not losing my salvation. But at the same time, every second of my life is not a spiritual one. I struggle." Denise said.

"Well we all do, it's because we live in this flesh. And stop claiming that you struggle child." Darlene said as Aunt Vye cell phone rung.

"Hello, yes? Maxine calm down. We'll be right there! Maxine relax, we're leaving right now!" Aunt Vye said.

"What happened?" Darlene asked Aunt Vye.

"What is it?" Sheryl said.

"Maxine said that Bryce decided to give your father one of his kidneys."

"Okay, that's great, but why do you look like something is wrong?" Sheryl asked.

"Cause' your Daddy's body rejected the kidney."

"What?" Darlene said.

"Well how is Dad doing? Did she say?" Sheryl asked.

"She said that Dad is not expected to make it another few hours and it doesn't look good for Bryce either."

"What you mean Bryce?" Darlene asked.

"What are we standing around for? Let's go." Sheryl said.

"We can't leave Joseph." Denise said.

"Well just call him and tell him to come back so that we all can catch a cab and get back over to the hospital."

Darlene said to Denise as she scrambled around to get herself together.

"Okay." Denise replied.

Accept Me Lord

I have never felt so much pain in my life as I was feeling now. I felt like the nurse's did not give me anything that would help me ease the pain for after the surgery. Everything from my chest down felt like it was on fire and I also couldn't feel my toes as I wiggled them. I actually thought that something was going to go wrong once the nurse pricked me at least four times on the back of my hand trying to find a good vein for the IV. All of this could not be the norm as my hands started to sweat and turn cold just as my back begin to stiffen up. I could see my life flashing in front of me. I saw me and my sisters on swings as my mother went to each one pushing us all. I could see my wife standing in a garden wearing a pretty white dress while holding some flowers and waiting for me to walk to her, but somehow I couldn't get my feet to move for me to get to her. I could hear Mama telling me to be strong as she prayed for me. And strangely of all I could hear my father calling out to God as if he was in the bed right next to me.

"God, I really, really, really need you right now. I need to accept you into my life! I'm calling on you right now. Lord please hear my cry, don't let me die today in front of my children. I am so sorry for causing a lifetime of hurt and pain. I'm sorry. Please forgive me Lord, I do believe in you now. I do believe in you now. I know that life can only be lived forwards, but now I understand it as I view it backwards. Father God, please don't walk away from me now when I need you the most. Please don't. Dear Lord I cannot change my past, but I can start a new beginning today. I cry out to you as I lay in this hospital bed to assure you that I now know that sometimes problems don't require a solution, they just need maturity involved to make it right. For years I didn't know what to do. It seems that no one understands me, and that no one cared to know my pain." Bryce could clearly hear in Dad's voice as he dozed off to sleep.

"Excuse me miss." A nurse says to Maxine who is pacing in the hallway while watching BJ eat some snacks in the waiting area room.

"Yes?" Maxine replied.

"Is Mr. King's children or family around?"

"No, but they should be here shortly. I called them about twenty minutes ago. Is there anything that I can do? I'm his daughter in law and that's my husband Bryce who you guys just did the surgery on."

"Well Mr. King is requesting a pastor at his bedside. He says he wants to repent for his sins."

"This is what he told you?"

"No, but he told one of the other nurses."

"Maxie I gotta' go to the bathroom and I gotta' go now." BJ said as he walked up to Maxine jumping around.

"Can you hold it?"

"No I can't."

"There's a bathroom right around that corner to the left." The nurse said to Maxine as she pointed down the hallway.

"Okay, let's go LB. Thank you so much Miss." Maxine said as she grabbed a hold of BJ's hand.

"Mrs. King, please bring the family to see me or Dr. Johnson once they arrive. Thank you." The nurse said as they slowly parted ways.

"I will."

"Bathroom Maxie please."

"Everything will be alright Mrs. King. And don't forget around the corner to the left for the young man." The nurse says as she checks her clipboard and the room number above the door before she enters to check on a patient.

"Thank you. I am praying and I have put it all in God's hands."

"I'm praying too. Can we find the bathroom please?" BJ asked as they walked down the hall to look for a bathroom.

"As a professional I am sorry." The nurse said as she stepped back out of the patient's room.

"Look let me get this young man to the bathroom. I believe in God's report. We will deal with everything else when the time is right." Maxine said as she again turned to walk off.

"So sorry." The nurse mumbled as she rearranged her head cap.

"Nurse, nurse. How come our father is not in his room?" Baby Boy screamed from down the hall.

"What's going on?" Sheryl asked as her and Baby Boy walked toward the nurse.

"Your father is in recovery. He is still in critical condition." The nurse replied as she walked toward the family.

"We would like to see him right now." Darlene said.

"Okay no problem. Let me page Dr. Johnson and also have some of the other nurses prep you all and then we can get you guys in there to see him. Come with me please." The nurse said as she led the family down the hallway.

"I want to see Dr. Johnson. I need to give him a piece of my mind." Sheryl said to the nurse as they trailed her.

"Sheryl not now. That is not going pull Dad or Bryce through." Darlene said as she pulled Sheryl to the side for a second.

"He messed up my brother and you telling me to play nice? No Darlene. I am not you and I will not sit here as they kill my brother." Sheryl said as she pulled her arm away from Darlene.

"I'm just saying. Let's find out what happened first before we jump to conclusions." Darlene said to Sheryl as she started to walk and catch up with Baby Boy and the nurse.

"Where is Maxine?" Aunt Vye asked as she met the group as they were walking down the hall behind with the nurse.

"Oh yes. Before the surgery your father had asked us could we have a pastor stop by his bedside to pray while he recovered." The nurse turned and said as they all approached the elevator bank.

"A Pastor? Yeah he must want to repent now." Baby Boy said as he watched the nurse press the up button on the wall for the elevator.

"Oh now that he's on his death bed he wants God." Sheryl said as she backed away from Darlene who was still jawing into her ear.

"Sheryl shut up. You starting to sound just like Daddy and Bryce. One minute your defending him and the next minute your tearing him down. You'd swallow your own blood before you swallow your own pride." Darlene said as Maxine and BJ turned the corner to walk up on them.

"Can you guys please keep an eye on this young man for me? I need to go down to ICU and check on my husband. And they won't allow BJ into the room with me." Maxine asked.

"Which way is recovery?" Aunt Vye asked.

"Recovery is on the fourth floor." The nurse said as the elevator door opened up.

"I'm coming wait." Aunt Vye said to the nurse as she entered the elevator.

"You all can meet me up there in five minutes." The nurse said to the family before the doors closed.

"Bryce is in ICU is on the second floor." Maxine said to Aunt Vye just as the elevator door closed.

"I'm coming with you Maxine." Baby Boy said.

"Give me a second alone with him first Joseph." Maxine said as she pressed the down button on the elevator.

"That's my brother." Baby Boy replied.

"Baby Boy." Darlene said.

"I want to see my brother." Baby Boy said as he looked at Darlene.

"And that's her husband. Let her have her time. Bryce is going to be alright, we all will see him." Darlene said to Baby Boy as she reached out to get BJ.

"LB you stay here with your Aunt's okay. I'll be right back." Maxine said as she put her hand on his head to walk him closer to Darlene.

"Okay Maxie." BJ said as they all looked at him in amazement.

"BJ, Lil' Bryce is that you?" Darlene asked as Maxine got on the elevator.

"Yes it's me."

"Boy come on over here and give your Aunt Darlene a big hug. Boy I haven't seen you since you were about 8 months old."

"Yeah you right, he does have Bryce's head." Sheryl said as she watch Darlene give BJ a nice long hug.

"We need to go and find Dad." Baby Boy said as she grabbed BJ by the head and pressed the elevator button.

"Yeah you're right. Call Denise and tell her to come upstairs because we need her to watch BJ so that we can go see Dad in recovery." Darlene said.

"Darlene look. Denise don't." Baby Boy said as he looked above the door to see which floor the elevator was on.

"Baby Boy now is not the time for what she do and what she don't do. Call her and tell her that we need her to come up here and take BJ downstairs with her so that we can go see Dad. What's so hard with doing that?" Darlene said as she raised her voice to get her point across.

"I'll take him downstairs to her. Come on BJ!" Baby Boy said to avoid having the discussion on the phone in front of his sisters.

"Meet us near Dad's room on the second floor on your way back up." Sheryl said as she pressed the elevator button twice.

"Okay. Come on BJ." Baby Boy said to BJ as they got on the elevator.

"Now what's your problem?" Sheryl asked Darlene as she stopped her from pressing the button.

"You're my problem. Our father is here dying right now and all you can do is be his judge and jury!" Darlene said as she turned around to walk back down the hallway.

"No not at all, but you're the one who said that Dad molested you." Sheryl said as she walked behind Darlene.

"Look neither one of us has a heaven or a hell to put anyone into. Dad has to answer for his sins and transgressions not you." Darlene said as she stopped and addressed Sheryl face to face.

"Yeah and that's why he wants a pastor now."

"Pray for him. If you're going to do anything for Dad, Can you at least pray for him?" Darlene said as she started to walk back towards the waiting area room.

"Oh I will, but he should've brought himself with us to church just like Mama asked him to. Mama always asked him to turn his life over to God or to at least show his face in the house of the Lord once in a while. But he chose otherwise. He chose to sit home and watch football every Sunday." Sheryl said as she walked behind Darlene down the hallway.

"I know what Mama said. I was there too Sheryl. I always play back Mama's words to myself." Darlene stopped to say.

"Girl's there is a thin line between here and heaven and a thinner line between here and hell. So come on kids, let's go on to church and get our dance on. Praise the lord. Yes, yes praise the lord. Because it is always good to have him and not need him, than to need him and not have him at all, and we going to get everything that God has for us." Mama would say.

"Amen. As I think back, Mama was always there for us." Darlene said as her and Sheryl sat down.

"Excuse me ladies, I regret to inform you that your father has passed on. My condolences, you have my deepest sympathy." Dr. Johnson said as he walked up slowly with his head hung low and pausing before speaking.

"No." Darlene cries as she sits down.

"I'm so sorry ladies. If there's anything that me or my staff can do.."

"Get away from us. Don't you think you and your staff did enough already! Get away." Sheryl screamed.

"I'm sorry you feel that way. I will send our ministerial staff to assist you all with anything that you may need." Dr. Johnson said before leaving.

"Don't send no staff, just get away." Sheryl said as she looked up at him.

"So sad, so sad. Father God, please lay your hands on this family. Shield them. Cover them in your blood. Father they truly, truly need you.

And Father please, please keep their brother in your closest care as he also fights to recover." The Homeless Lady prayed from her seat as she pointed towards Sheryl and Darlene.

"Thank you so much Ms. Maxwell." Darlene sat up and said as she wiped away her tears.

"I really hope I wasn't out of place, but I allowed a close friend of mine, who is also a pastor and a secretary here to lay hands and counsel your father at his bedside!"

The Homeless Lady said as she walked closer to Sheryl and Darlene.

"Thank you again Ms. Maxwell for your kind words. Thank you for all that you've done." Darlene said as she tried to hold back her tears.

"Your welcome."

"Darlene tell me it's not true. Tell me Daddy's not gone." Sheryl screamed out as Darlene then hugged her tighter.

"It's going to be alright Sheryl. It's going to be alright." Darlene said as she rocked her and Sheryl both back and forth.

"No. Darlene please tell me no. Please tell me no. What did they do to him?" Sheryl cried out as she laid in Darlene's arms.

"My brother, my brother." Aunt Vye screamed as she walked in crying.

"Aunt Vye." Darlene screamed out as she cried.

"My brother. My brother." Aunt Vye cried out as she stood motionless in the doorway.

"Come here Auntie." Darlene said to Aunt Vye as Maxine walked up behind her crying and shaking.

"How is Bryce?" Darlene asked a visibly bothered Maxine.

"They messed up, they messed him up!" Maxine replied as Aunt Vye grabbed her from falling.

"What do you mean they messed him up?" Sheryl asked as she sat up from Darlene's lap.

"My baby. The surgery. He may never be able to walk again. They did something wrong!" Maxine said as her and Aunt Vye walked over to the bench seat to sit down.

"What you mean they did something wrong?" Darlene asked.

"Where is he at? What room is he in?" Sheryl asked as she stood up, wiped and sucked back her tears.

"We need to see him." Aunt Vye said.

"He's not even conscience. They asked me to step out of his room about twenty minutes ago so they could work on him." Maxine said as Aunt Vye held onto her in the seat.

"No. This can't be happening." Darlene said to Maxine as she stood up and walked over to her.

"I'm going down there. I don't trust them for another second with my brother." Sheryl said as she got up to walk out.

"He doesn't even know about Dad." Darlene said as Bryce is being rolled into the waiting area room in a wheelchair by a nurse.

"Bryce!" screamed Sheryl.

"Baby you okay." Maxine said as she jumped up to run over to him.

"Bryce what happened?" Darlene asked.

"My life. Life happened. Being just like Daddy happened, holding a grudge against him and allowing my heart to remain dark and heavy with hate happened. I should have forgiven him. And now, now it's too late for me to make peace within' myself and with him."

"Did they tell you about your father?" Aunt Vye asked as she turned in her chair.

"Yes I was told. Look I need you all to stay close and to look out for BJ." Bryce said as the nurse pushed him further into the waiting room.

"Bryce you are going to be okay. What are you talking about?" Maxine said as she kneeled down next to him.

"You ladies got him?" The nurse asked.

"Yes we do." Darlene and Maxine replied.

"I'm not going to be okay." Bryce said as he grunted and moved his body to reposition it in the wheelchair as the nurse walked off.

"Be careful." Maxine said as she tried to help him.

"Please don't talk like that." Sheryl said as she and walked over to him.

"What about BJ's mother? Doesn't he live with her?" Darlene asked as she walked to the side of the wheelchair next to Maxine.

"Yes, but he's still my son, your family, our blood. And now he's a son to you Maxine, to you all" Bryce says with a few coughs in his sentence.

"No Bryce. You will be okay." Maxine said as she rubbed his back.

"HE IS A PIECE OF ME." Bryce said.

"Bryce you're going to be fine, and you will help raise BJ along with his mother and us." Sheryl said as she kneeled down and rubbed his hand that still had the butterfly band aid and the IV attachment on it.

"Look, I just want you guys to keep a close eye on my boy. Just try to stay in his life for me. Make sure that he turns out to be better than me and his grandfather."

"Everything will be alright. You will be there to help raise your son. You have to think positive." Darlene said as she tried to close the back of his gown.

"Excuse me King Family, your brother Joseph just walked into your father's room and he is going crazy. He just found out about your father. Can you all come and help?" A nurse running in asked.

"What. Nobody told him." Aunt Vye said as she ran out behind Sheryl.

"We need all of your help, he's going crazy. Please come quick before the hospital police hurt him." The nurse said.

"Bryce." Darlene said as she looked at him before running out.

"Go. Go make sure Baby Boy is alright! I'll be okay right here with my wife." Bryce said to Darlene as she paused before going to help with Baby Boy.

"Are you sure?" Darlene asked.

"Yes. Go."

"Okay. We'll be right back Maxine." Darlene said as she kissed Bryce on the top of his head and rushed out.

"I got him Darlene, go ahead." Maxine said as she rubbed Bryce's head.

"This pain is no joke." Bryce said as he frowned and shifted in the wheelchair.

"Where does it hurt?"

"Where doesn't it hurt is more like the question. Max' can you please run down that hallway and get me a bottle of water out of that machine."

"Bryce I'm not leaving you here or letting you out of my sight. I can roll you right to that machine with me." Maxine said as she looked into his eyes.

"Max' I felt every bump that we hit coming down that hallway. Can you get me some water please. My mouth is so dry." Bryce said as he looked back at Maxine.

"Okay. You sure you don't want me to.."

"Water babe, please."

"Alright I will be right back." Maxine said as she stood up to check into her pockets for some money.

"Thanks babe." Bryce said as he licked his dry chapped lips.

"You welcome. But let me move you over there out of the way." Maxine said as she slowly moved him out of the walkway.

"Slow." Bryce said as his face grimaced.

"I got you. There you go." Maxine said as she turned and rested the back of the wheelchair up against the wall.

"Thank you." Bryce said as he sunk into the wheel-chair.

"You sure you don't want to go?" Maxine asked as she pointed towards the doorway.

"Thank you babe. I will be right here." Bryce said as his eyes followed Maxine out before closing them and leaning his head back to relax.

"Boy wake yourself up, get up! Get up boy, before you miss something." Daddy King said as he stood over Bryce while tapping him on his shoulder.

"Bryce, pull yourself together and let's go. Maxine's contractions are getting closer and closer in there." Mama said as she sat next to him on the bench seat.

"Boy your wife is about to have this baby!" Daddy King said as Bryce jumped up and wiped his eyes.

"What, What? Who? Mama, Dad, y'all alright. Your alive? Thank God." Bryce screamed as he reached out to touch Daddy King's face.

"What do you mean we alright, we alive? Boy what you talking about, of course we alive. You can see me can't you?" Daddy King said as he smacked Bryce's hand away from his face.

"Joseph Sr. stop that." Mama said as she rubbed Bryce's head.

"Joseph Sr. nothing he better come on with these dumb questions. Are we alive? Yeah we alive. Does a crowded elevator smell different to a midget? Daddy King said as he put one knee onto the bench seat.

"You are not helping the situation Joseph." Mama said as Daddy King leaned down over Bryce to look into his pupils.

"Boy get up and get into that room and make this happen. Got me here at this hospital for no reason. Knowing they got a Good Times marathon on this weekend and you know how I loves me some Wilona. How you gon' get nauseous as your wife is having your first child?" Daddy King said as he pulled on Bryce's arm.

"My baby just got a little overwhelmed. Leave him alone." Mama said as she swung her purse at Daddy King to move him away from Bryce.

"Leave him alone. He better man up." Daddy King said as he backed up and wiped around his mouth.

"Joseph King Sr. cut it out.."

"No it's just crazy. I had the craziest dream that you two were dead. Mom you had passed already and Dad was here at this hospital sick and dying. Darlene was crying and making accusations, well I don't want to go into all of that. And Sheryl and Aunt Vye', well they were Sheryl and Aunt Vye'." Bryce said as Mama grabbed and held his hand.

"You see, now I know this is your child, sick so quick and crazy when he hazy. He has to be on that stuff. This is what I'm talking about when I said that you should've been boiling that tap water that you put into the milk for our kids." Daddy King said as he put his fingers to his mouth as if he was smoking.

"Joseph go sit somewhere and be quiet. Earth to Bryce. Earth to Bryce, we are at this hospital because your wife is in labor with your daughter. Come on and pull it together. You know these babies don't wait on nobody, you better hurry it up. Plus I got a revival service tonight at my church, boy let's get go."

"Where are they?" Bryce asked.

"They in the room, where you need to be." Daddy King screamed out from across the room.

"These babies come when they wanna' come. Chile' I don't know what these women are eating these days." Mama said.

"So now get in there and induce this labor so I can go home and finish watching me some "Good times…,hanging in the chow line.."" Daddy King said as he walked back over to Bryce and Mama.

"Joseph, you so busy worried about seeing Wilona when you need to be concerned about your first grand being born."

"I'm joking Josey, lighten up, don't tighten up." Daddy King said and danced over to Maxine as she was being wheeled into the waiting area room in a wheelchair with the newborn baby.

"Uh oh, somebody done missed something." Mama said.

"Is that my baby with my baby?" Bryce said as he jumped up to walk towards Maxine in the wheelchair.

"Here we are sweetie your two favorite girls." Maxine said as the nurse pushing the wheelchair came to a stop.

"Maxine, I love you and I am so sorry. You are my best friend and my wife. I will forever remain honest to you. I promise you that nothing has changed." Bryce said as he kneeled down to look at Maxine as she stopped him from opening up the baby's blanket.

"Bryce what are you talking about? And what happened to you helping me breathe and push? You left out the room to get some air and you never came back, what happened?"

"Well I.."

"What, you couldn't find the air? Don't even answer. I just need you to make it back down to my room so that you can hold your daughter because I carried her long enough, and I am tired." Maxine said as she covered the baby up some more.

"I'm dirty babe. Let's go back to the room and let me get a cover to put over me and I will hold her all day and night." Bryce said as he stood up.

"It's too many germs out here. Push me to my room please."

"Let me hold her because I still have my cover on." Mama said.

"You sure can hold her Mama. But please push me back down to my room so that I can get back into that bed and then you can hold your grandchild for as long as you want."

"That's alright with me. Now put your feet up and let's get to rolling." Mama said as she turned the wheelchair around and pushed them out.

"Wait for us." Bryce said as he looked and smiled at Daddy King.

"We see y'all in a minute." Maxine said as Mama pushed them out.

"Dad I tell you this is the greatest feeling in the world. My first born, I'm about to go and hold my first born." Bryce said as he walked back over to get Maxine's belongings off of the bench seat.

"Yes it is son, a great feeling. Trust me there is no greater feeling in this world than when you hold your child for the first time." Daddy King said as he grabbed Bryce by the shoulder.

"This is unbelievable, I'm a father now." Bryce said as he hugged his father.

"Enjoy it son, soak it up. I remember the first time I held you. Boy your head was so heavy." Daddy King said to Bryce as the stood face to face with his hands on each of Bryce's shoulder.

"Come on Dad, you not even funny." Bryce said as he faked a punch into his father's stomach.

"It's true though." Daddy King said as he moved back.

"Dad my brother John, your first born. I never, ever, really asked you about him because I was a teenager, but how did you deal with losing your child to drugs? Especially as a pastor?" Bryce asked as they started to walk out before stopping.

"You know what Bryce, I was mad. I was mad as a father. I was even mad as a pastor. I was mad at God. I cursed him. I cursed at him and I even screamed to the heavens. I can stand here now and seriously tell you that I contemplated walking away from God at that point." he said with tears in his eyes as he placed his hand on Bryce's shoulder.

"You thought about not preaching anymore?"

"I sure did. But then I sat down and had a conversation with God and I asked him. Where was he at when I needed him most? I asked him where was he at in my time of need?"

"Did he answer you?"

"Bryce, I got on my knees and I asked God. After all you've shown me, where were you at when my son died? And Bryce I tell you I heard a voice out of nowhere say to me."

"SON, I WAS IN THE SAME PLACE WHEN YOUR SON DIED AS I WAS WHEN MY SON JESUS CHRIST DIED. I WILL NEVER EVER LEAVE YOU, EVEN WHEN YOU LEAVE ME. FOR YOU ARE A PIECE OF ME AS I AM A PIECE OF YOU."

A Piece of Me